He _____ ___ ___ ___ ses with his nearness. Dark curling hairs covered the wide expanse of his upper chest. The towel draped across his hard shoulders did nothing to hide his physique. In the deep shadows of the hallway his features were the outline of male menace. But his green eyes were clearly visible, a tender longing blazing in them.

Liz stared at him, all too aware of the towel that barely covered his hips. Her nostrils were filled with the scent of subtle cologne and male flesh, and she couldn't speak.

"I don't think I want to know where you were going," he murmured, "but you were headed in the right direction for what I have in mind."

A hard shaft of desire shot through her, trapping Liz as effectively as his body did. She realized the little girl in her had brewed plenty of mischief tonight, but now only the woman was left, helplessly responding to this man. . . .

WHAT ARE *LOVESWEPT* ROMANCES?

They are stories of true romance and touching emotion. We believe those two very important ingredients are constants in our highly sensual and very believable stories in the *LOVESWEPT* line. Our goal is to give you, the reader, stories of consistently high quality that may sometimes make you laugh, sometimes make you cry, but are always fresh and creative and contain many delightful surprises within their pages.

Most romance fans read an enormous number of books. Those they truly love, they keep. Others may be traded with friends and soon forgotten. We hope that each *LOVESWEPT* romance will be a treasure—a "keeper." We will always try to publish

LOVE STORIES YOU'LL NEVER FORGET
BY AUTHORS YOU'LL ALWAYS REMEMBER

The Editors

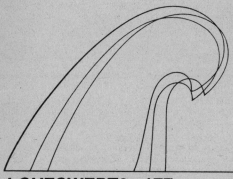

LOVESWEPT® • 177

Linda Cajio
Hard Habit to Break

BANTAM BOOKS
TORONTO • NEW YORK • LONDON • SYDNEY • AUCKLAND

HARD HABIT TO BREAK

A Bantam Book / January 1987

*LOVESWEPT® and the wave device are registered
trademarks of Bantam Books, Inc. Registered in U.S. Patent
and Trademark Office and elsewhere.*

Cover art by Walter Popp.

*If you would be interested in receiving protective vinyl
covers for your Loveswept books, please write to this address
for information:*

*Loveswept
Bantam Books
P.O. Box 985
Hicksville, NY 11802*

ISBN 0-553-21802-6

Published simultaneously in the United States and Canada

*Bantam Books are published by Bantam Books, Inc. Its trade-
mark, consisting of the words "Bantam Books" and the por-
trayal of a rooster, is Registered in U.S. Patent and Trademark
Office and in other countries. Marca Registrada. Bantam
Books, Inc., 666 Fifth Avenue, New York, New York 10103.*

PRINTED IN THE UNITED STATES OF AMERICA

O   0 9 8 7 6 5 4 3 2 1

For John and Genna—my angels, my devils.
I wish you two would make up your minds.
All my love, Mom.

One

"Does your mother know you smoke?"

The cigarette raised halfway to her lips, Liz O'Neal spun in the direction of the deep and disapproving male voice. Her dismay and surprise turned to shock when she caught sight of the man standing on the other side of the waist-high boxwood hedge.

He was naked.

At least he looked that way, she thought. Staring slack-jawed at the glistening bronze skin, she told herself that her new neighbor couldn't possibly be attempting to bring Michelangelo's *David* to life. Most likely he was wearing a pair of shorts against the unusually steamy afternoon heat. She hoped. Nudity and northern Vermont's normally cool summers didn't exactly go hand in hand.

But the abnormal eighty-five-degree temperature seemed to have risen one hundred points in the last minute.

Liz moaned to herself as her gaze traveled helplessly up and down the gorgeous torso. Her heart thumped at a supersonic pace. From what she could see, the statue had a long way to go before it matched her neighbor.

He peered down his Roman nose at her, topping her five feet two inches by at least another foot. His face was lean, the cheekbones high and well-defined, and the short mahogany-brown beard he wore did nothing to hide the square jaw or the firmness of his lips. Long thick lashes fringed the greenest eyes she'd ever seen. His dark hair was liberally streaked by the sun, the loose curls precision-cut and brushed back off his broad forehead—except for a few rebellious locks that dipped forward.

Her hypnotized eyes shifted to the strong neck that flowed into broad shoulders. Farther down, they discovered a heavy pelt of silky hair covering his chest and torso. The damn hedge effectively hid the rest of him.

Liz swallowed, suddenly grateful for the barrier separating them. She didn't think she could take any more perfection, dressed or, especially, undressed. She didn't want to know for sure.

"I'm glad to see you won't be smoking that cigarette," he said, his eyes focused on her now clenched hands. "I'm sorry I startled you. But if you promise to stop sneaking cigarettes behind the shed, I promise not to tell your mother."

His words broke her trance, and Liz glanced down at the cigarette she'd inadvertently crushed.

"Dammit!" She felt a hot flush staining her cheeks.

"Honey, you're not going to grow up any faster by cursing and smoking. Just be yourself."

Liz glared at Mr. America's tolerantly smiling face. "I am not a child—"

"Of course you're not," he broke in with a soothing tone. "But don't rush nature; it'll all come soon enough anyway. And you won't ruin your lungs in the process."

"But . . ."

Holding up a hand to stop her words, he added, "Be smart and give it up. Believe me, I don't want to tell your mother about your smoking. I know what it's like to be a teenager and want to be an adult. You've already got a great head start, and in a few more years—"

Her barely held temper broke, and Liz stalked over to the hedge. She jabbed the Adonis in the chest with a finger.

"Will you shut your self-righteous mouth and listen to me? I'm not a kid anymore. I'm twenty-seven years old, and I'll smoke wherever and whenever I damn well please."

His eyes momentarily widened in surprise, and she gave him a smug smile, satisfied that she had brought his lecture to a complete and total halt.

"I'm sorry. I thought you were about fifteen." His gaze leisurely lowered to her slender figure clad in very short cutoff jeans and a yellow tube top. He grinned, his teeth gleaming whitely against his beard. "For a moment I wondered if teenage girls were maturing faster than they did in my day. But you still shouldn't smoke."

Liz opened her mouth to yell, and immediately shut it. Turning on her heel, she marched around the shed and across the wide velvety expanse of grass to her large Dutch colonial house.

She was not about to explain her method of kicking the habit to him. Down to three cigarettes a day, she had made a so far unbroken rule to smoke them only at specific times and places during the day. Her plan had been working beautifully, but, because of that . . . that walking statue she had missed one and couldn't have another until nine that night. Seven hours without a cigarette! Chinese water torture sounded like a vacation idyll compared to that. Skipping a cigarette might be good for her health but not for her already frayed disposition.

And now she was living next door to Dear Abby.

Matt Callahan grinned self-deprecatingly to himself as his neighbor's back door slammed shut. He'd just made a mess of meeting her, but he was more than grateful she *wasn't* fifteen.

It was an understandable error, he acknowledged wryly. When he'd caught his first glimpse of her, furtively huddled behind the shed, he'd naturally assumed her small, delicate frame was still undergoing the maturing process. The heavy wheat-blond hair pulled back in a ponytail had only enhanced his impression of child-woman. And the shock at being discovered had been very evident in her wide gray eyes, so he'd been sure she was a teenager. It wasn't until she'd exploded in anger that he'd realized what a delightful mistake he'd made.

Her cheekbones had flushed a deep pink, emphasizing the myriad pale freckles dotting her face. Her chin had shot up to a very stubborn angle, and her full lips had pursed. He'd immediately wanted to feel them with his. She had looked so naturally seductive, and it was obvious a very passionate nature lurked beneath her ingenue exterior. He definitely wanted to know his next door neighbor better. Much better.

Hopewell, Vermont, wasn't quite the peaceful small town he'd been expecting. Not when it had neighbors like her, whoever she was.

An unwanted thought occurred to him, and he grimaced. He hoped she wasn't married, although her smoking behind the shed indicated she was hiding her habit from someone.

Taking a deep breath of sweet-smelling air, Matt glanced up at the bright, cloudless sky and decided to do some yardwork instead of more unpacking. The house had been empty for several months, so the yard was overgrown. And being retired now, he really should cultivate a hobby. Gardening was nice. Besides, there was the added advantage of spotting a husband if there was one.

And if there wasn't one, he intended to spend a good deal of time next door.

Maybe he ought to cut a hole in the hedge. "Accidentally," of course.

Seven hours later Liz gazed at the lone cigarette lying in splendor on the top of her white-pine coffee table.

Picking it up, she silently cursed as she remembered what had happened to her last cigarette.

Damn that man! She'd started smoking behind the shed so she'd feel foolish and embarrass herself into cutting down to two cigarettes a day. But she hadn't ever expected to be caught at it, like a teenager.

Remembering her instant attraction to the man across the hedge, she groaned loudly. Why did he have to be the healthiest male specimen this side of the Green Mountains? And why did he have to move in next door to her?

It had been over two years since her painful, pride-bruising divorce. She'd finally straightened out her life. She didn't want a man. She didn't *need* a man. So why did she have a heart-stopping, gooey-eyed reaction to him?

"Because he's gorgeous," she muttered out loud. "Big deal."

She acknowledged, though, that she'd been somewhat rude to him, and she'd felt a little guilty about it ever since. Good thing she wasn't a Welcome Wagon lady, or she'd be out of a job.

Liz grimaced in frustration, suddenly realizing how much her own job as bank manager depended on good public relations with the community. She only hoped she hadn't blown a new account. Actually, she was pretty sure she hadn't. After all, the Hopewell branch of the New England Bank was the only bank for fifteen miles in any direction. From now on, though, she would be friendly yet a little distant to her new neighbor. She didn't want the town gossips to have any mistaken impressions about her relationship with him. It wasn't every day Hopewell got a new citizen, and speculation would be intense. They'd both be under the microscope for a long time.

Liz groaned again. Knowing Hopewell, they'd be under it forever.

She firmly reminded herself she'd missed having her afternoon cigarette. It had taken monumental willpower not to run to her purse and get another. She silently congratulated herself and added a footnote to forget about her neighbor. He could be trouble, and for more than one reason. She didn't need any more worries, especially now.

Rolling the smooth cigarette between her fingers, she sighed thankfully. At least she'd be able to smoke this one.

Just as she was raising the cigarette to her lips, her doorbell rang. Surprised that someone in Hopewell would actually be out at nine in the evening, even on a Sunday night, Liz self-consciously cupped the cigarette in her hand to hide it. Then she walked across the federal blue carpeting of her living room to answer the bell.

Opening the darkly stained door, Liz gaped. Staring at a wide, T-shirt-covered chest, she dimly wondered if her neighbor had a thing about clothes. Besides the T-shirt, he wore only his beard, a pair of rubber thongs on his feet, and cutoff jeans faded almost white. They seemed to outline rather than cover the essentials.

"Hi. I'm Matt Callahan. I'm really sorry about what happened this afternoon, and I wanted to apologize."

Her eyes still focused three feet below his face, Liz nodded absently. His voice sounded as if he were in the next state. Maybe she was getting a cold, and her ears were stopped up.

"Can I ask a favor?"

"Anything," she blurted out hoarsely, then nearly gasped in horror at her answer. Glancing up sharply, she saw no change in his politely smiling face. She cleared her throat, hoping he hadn't heard her. "Yes, of course."

His smile broadened as he held up a yellow stoneware sugar bowl. "Can I borrow some sugar for tomorrow's breakfast? I need a morning eye-opener, and I haven't yet found the box that has the kitchen stuff."

The request was innocent enough, and it was a good opportunity to make up for her initial rudeness to him.

Liz smiled, reaching out to accept the bowl. She immediately caught sight of shredded tobacco and paper in her now open palm.

"My cigarette!" She moaned loudly.

Hooking his little finger through the sugar bowl handle, Matt took her hand and pulled her the few steps over the threshold and onto the porch.

"You shouldn't be smoking these filthy things," he said while brushing her hand clean.

Liz snatched her hand away and made an inhuman sound in her throat before shouting, "I can't take it anymore!"

She stalked back inside the house to the mirrored coat rack next to the door. Grabbing her tan canvas purse, she rummaged through it and pulled out a pack of cigarettes and matches.

"Don't light it," Matt warned as he entered the house.

Liz's slender control over her rising anger broke. Repeating the earlier confrontation, her finger poked him again in the chest. "I was doing very well until you moved next door! Now leave my cigarettes alone and mind your own business, Mr. Aerobics!"

"I guess this means no sugar."

She ignored him. She lit the cigarette and inhaled deeply, her withdrawal symptoms already disappearing. Closing her eyes and leaning against the coat rack, she took another satisfying drag.

"I hate to admit it," he said, "but you look like you needed that."

Liz blinked and straightened. Her screaming nerves finally soothed, she felt more charitable toward her unwanted devil's advocate. Smiling happily, she said, "I've been very rude to you, haven't I? I'm sorry. You see, I'm trying to quit, and I'm down to three cigarettes a day."

"None is better."

She eyed him for a long moment, tempted to stuff her purse into his mouth. So much for charity. "Three are better than thirty."

He grinned ruefully and nodded in understanding. "Good point. Congratulations."

He stretched out a hand, and Liz met it with hers. A strange tingling warmth suddenly radiated up her arm, and she forgot how to speak.

"Lived here long?" he asked, his green eyes seeming to turn even greener. He didn't shake her hand, only held it tightly.

Trying to unscramble the confusion in her brain so she could get her voice working again, she shook her head.

"Married?"

"Divorced."

It was a croaked answer, but she was grateful for any sound. She couldn't believe she was acting like a teenager *again*. Maybe she ought to have her pituitary gland checked.

"Good," he murmured.

She shook her head again, positive she hadn't heard him correctly. Something was definitely wrong with her body.

"You haven't told me your name yet," he said in a louder voice.

She forced down the dizziness swirling inside her, and managed to reply, "Liz. Liz O'Neal."

"Liz. I'm sure we'll be the best of neighbors. How about coming over for dinner on Tuesday night so we can become better acquainted?"

Matt finally released her hand, and Liz felt her body return almost to normal. Then she panicked at his words. Best of neighbors, when he looked like God's example of the perfect male? Dinner? Better acquainted?

Suddenly she lost all desire for the cigarette she'd been so desperate for. She walked over to a small candlestick table by the stairs and stubbed it out in an ashtray.

She wryly admitted that if she stayed in Matt's immediate vicinity much longer, she'd be cured of her cigarette addiction before the week was out. It was one hell of a way to quit. She ordered her body to act its age. It was true that Matt was a good-looking and charming man, but she'd invested too much time already in maintaining her spotless image as a single woman and bank manager in a very small town. Granted, it had been easy so far, but if she saw Matt other than to nod a hello as next door neighbors, she might as well repeat Lady Godiva's ride around Hopewell's common. The results would be the same.

It was time to let him know exactly what kind of neighbor she wanted to be.

Turning, she drew herself upright and said in formal tones, "I believe you wanted some sugar."

"Only if you're willing to give it," he replied with a boyish grin.

His grin turned downward, though, when he realized Liz might take his remark as an innuendo. He held out the bowl and added, "I'd really appreciate it."

Taking the bowl, she made no comment and turned toward the kitchen.

Matt grimaced as he watched her walk away. Dammit! He really thought he was making some progress with her. All afternoon he'd been outside working on his yard. She'd never reappeared. But at least he'd seen no husband or boyfriend, and had finally decided to confirm his hopeful conclusion that Liz O'Neal was unattached.

Her gamine face and figure and her explosive emotions were an intriguing combination. Matt was already very attracted to her, and he wasn't about to miss an opportunity to explore further. But evidently she didn't feel the same way about him.

Matt dryly acknowledged he'd had no trouble attracting women in the past. In fact, after his adolescent delight at discovering how his looks enhanced his appeal to women, he'd realized it was only his face and body that interested the opposite sex. And his former profession had added to their assessment of him as an unintelligent man. Male models were supposedly all body and no brains. He'd acquired a healthy fortune on the side, predicting and investing in commodity futures, but his accomplishments had made no difference to most women. To them it was luck and not his long hours of research into weather conditions, the market, and government directives that had made him successful.

It had been years since he had wanted a woman to like him for his physical appearance. But he wished Liz did. At this point he wasn't above using any and everything to get a positive reaction from her.

"Here's your sugar," she said as she walked back into the room.

Smiling broadly, he took the filled bowl from her. "Thanks. You're a life saver."

She smiled back, and he decided to do his damnedest to insure they'd be more than just neighbors.

"How about steak on the grill?" he asked.

She blinked. "Steak?"

"Or chicken. Whatever you want."

"What are you talking about?"

He chuckled. "Dinner on Tuesday. Bring your empty stomach, and I'll burn something on the grill."

"Ahh . . . dinner." Her cheeks seemed more rosy, and she shifted her eyes away from him for an instant before adding, "That's very kind, Mr. Callahan. . . ."

"Matt."

"Matt. But you've probably got a lot of unpacking to do."

"And dinner with you will be a nice break." He reached out and took her hand, then lifted it to his lips and gallantly kissed the back of it. "Have pity on an overworked man, Liz, and come to dinner."

"But . . ."

"I promise not to say a word if you smoke."

"It isn't that—"

"Good. Three a day is quite an accomplishment after thirty."

He turned her hand over and planted another kiss on her sensitive palm. To his elation, he heard a tiny moan from deep in her throat. She did feel something too. But he also sensed she was holding back. He wondered if her divorce had left deep scars that he'd have to overcome.

Suddenly and fiercely he wanted to remove those scars and insure she would never have an unhappy moment again. Then another equally strong urge shot through him. He'd love to punch her ex-husband in the mouth.

His violent reaction took him by surprise, and he kissed her hand again, tasting the soft skin more fully this time. He raised his head and gazed into her wide gray eyes.

"Dinner on Tuesday, Liz. I absolutely insist."

She hesitated, and Matt knew if he gave her a chance, she'd say no. He quickly walked over to the front door.

"Thanks again for the sugar. I'll see you at seven on Tuesday."

He stepped outside and shut the door behind him, not noticing the swaying curtains at three houses across the street. He grinned into the dark night and half-ran across the lawn to his large gingerbread-laced Victorian home.

Maybe he'd cut that hole in the hedge tomorrow.

Two

"He's gorgeous!"

Seated behind her desk, Liz bent her head even lower toward her paperwork and moaned silently. Her own words had returned to haunt her. Her bank tellers had gossiped all morning about Matt, and they were still at it.

"I wonder why he's not married," one said.

"Maybe he's divorced," another replied.

"Maybe he just wants a weekend place in the country. We've got lots of part-timers around here."

"Who cares? He's the handsomest man to ever live in Hopewell. Part-timer or not."

Firmly ignoring the growing urge to scream, Liz prayed they'd stop soon. They had to stop talking about Matt sometime, she thought without much hope. And she couldn't reprimand them for it. She'd always allowed the girls to chat together as long as they waited on the customers and did their paperwork right. To speak to them now about gossiping would only have them wondering what was wrong with *her*.

It wouldn't take them very long to find the answer. Liz sighed, knowing she was trapped. It was enough to make her want a cigarette.

Her gaze remained unfocused on the deposit reports she was supposed to be coordinating for the bank's central office in Swanton. She wished she had a whole pack of cigarettes in her hands. She'd light all twenty at once. Tonight she had to face Matt and tell him she *wasn't* dining with him tomorrow evening.

Groaning in self-disgust this time, Liz had a sure feeling she'd be reduced to oatmeal again. What was the matter with her anyway? Why couldn't she seem to act like a mature adult around him? Okay, so he was good-looking, and charming, and sexy . . .

In her mind's eye she could see Matt as he stood behind the hedge. She could almost feel the dense swath of hair on his chest. It would be like silk under her hands. And the skin that glistened like oiled oak in the sunlight would be smooth and damp—

"Hi, Liz."

Her wits scattered at the sound of an already too familiar voice speaking her name. She glanced up in shock to find the object of her erotic daydream standing before her.

This time, at least, Matt was completely dressed. But his loose white cotton shirt with the sleeves rolled to just below his elbows emphasized a multitude of perfections. The broad shoulders seemed broader, the hard chest harder, and the trim waist even trimmer. The beige pleated trousers he wore were the latest male fashion.

Not only was Matt Callahan charismatic and virile, he had style too.

Telling herself she couldn't possibly have conjured him off the pages of *Esquire* magazine and into the bank, Liz tried to compose herself into a semblance of normalcy. As she stood, her shaking legs told her normal was impossible. She decided to try for semi-idiocy.

"Hello, Mr. Callahan," she said, surprised at the strong formal tone of her voice. She'd been so sure she'd sound like a croaking frog again. To her left, she caught a glimpse of Georgina and Mavis leaning forward over the marble counter, obviously intent on hearing every word. "May I help you?"

Matt shot her a puzzled look. "I thought we'd gotten to first names last night."

Liz instantly wished the bank's roof would collapse on them. A hurricane blow through town. A bomb go off in City Hall across the street. Anything!

The silence was deafening.

So much for positive thinking, she decided after one hope-filled moment.

"I'm sorry . . . Matt," she replied hastily, thinking fast to disarm the bomb he'd innocently tossed her. "When you stopped by so briefly last night, I didn't get a chance to welcome you to Hopewell. Welcome to Hopewell. Is there something *the bank* can do for you this morning?"

Leaning his hand on her desk, Matt grinned. "It seems we forgot to talk about a lot of things last night."

Liz wondered wildly if the man was trying to sabotage her reputation. There wasn't anything he could say to make the situation worse.

"You didn't mention you worked at the bank," he went on. "Thanks again for your sweet contribution to my morning. I don't know what I would have done without it," he added with an even wider grin.

Her stomach lurching, Liz cursed silently. She'd been optimistic in thinking the situation couldn't be worse. Somehow Matt, in his innocence, had found a way to make her sound almost like the town hooker.

Maybe she was reading more into his words than anyone else might. After all, she was nervous and on edge with him, she reasoned.

Mentally crossing her fingers, she shifted her gaze over Matt's shoulder. Georgina's and Mavis's eyes were popping, and if they leaned over the counter any farther, they'd slide right down to the floor.

"Dammit!" Liz muttered, looking around for a mousehole to crawl into.

"What?" Matt asked with a blank look.

Suddenly she was furious with him, the nosy tellers, and a job that practically required her to walk on water. But she resisted the urge to vent her frustration. Her job was important to her, not only for income but also for her self-esteem. Granted walking on water wasn't a listed job requirement, but she'd do it if she had to. And everybody in a small town took an interest in everybody else. That was only human nature.

And that's the way it is, she told herself. Walter Cronkite really knew how to turn a phrase.

She gave a very saccharine smile, first to Matt and then to the tellers. "I don't like black coffee either, so I was glad to lend you the sugar. Now I assume you're not here to return what you borrowed and want to open an account with the bank."

Matt chuckled. "Ah . . . a mind reader."

"Lucky guess. Please have a seat." She glared at Georgina and Mavis, who suddenly began shuffling papers.

Still chuckling, Matt sat down in one of the two chrome and vinyl chairs on the other side of her desk. "Actually I do want to transfer some of my money up here for a household account."

Sitting back down in her chair, Liz pulled a new-accounts application and money transfer form from a drawer and laid it on the desk. Picking up a pen, she gazed expectantly at Matt with what she hoped was a businesslike expression. Now that she wasn't concerned with the tellers, her glands were beginning to work overtime again.

"I'll need to ask a few questions for our records and call your bank to confirm your account. The money should take no longer than twenty-four hours to be transferred here. But there won't be any problem if you need to cash a check today." Liz congratulated herself for not betraying her internal state with her voice.

"I can wait," Matt replied, his green eyes focused unwaveringly on her face. "Go ahead with the questions, Liz. I know I'm in good hands."

His words provoked an unwanted but very vivid

picture in Liz's mind. She instantly suppressed it and sternly told herself, Just get the interview over with, and get him out of here!

He answered her questions easily until she asked about his occupation.

"Retired," he said after a moment's hesitation.

Surprised, she stared at him. Retired? He couldn't be in his mid-thirties yet. Then a thought occurred to her. Vermont was a haven for executive types who were tired of the cities and wanted a change of lifestyles. Most were would-be writers, or artists, or gentleman farmers. Maybe Matt was one of those.

"I mean your occupation now."

"Watching you."

She blinked, not believing she'd heard him correctly. She wondered briefly if she would always have a hearing problem around him.

"Do you have a source of income?" she asked.

"If I'm lucky. By the way, I mowed your lawn this morning."

"You what!"

"Well, I was mowing mine, and noticed yours needed a haircut too. Think of it as repayment for the cup of sugar you lent me."

"You mowed my lawn." She closed her eyes, vowing to run over him with her car. Mowing her lawn sounded so damn intimate to her image-sensitive ears. Matt Callahan was driving her crazy.

"Here, let me do that," he said, and he gently pulled the papers and pen from her frozen hands.

She opened her eyes and, with helpless fatalism, watched as he quickly filled out the rest of the two forms. He slid them back to her.

Glancing down at the papers, she noted with a wry smile that *Retired* filled the occupation blank. Her eyes widened slightly when she read his current accounts were with a prestigious international New York bank. But her mouth dropped open, when she read the amount being transferred. Matt Callahan, who was rapidly becoming her personal nemesis, was about to become her largest private depositor.

"Everything okay?" he asked.

The figure had to be wrong. It was the only coherent thought running through her panic-stricken brain. She might have to watch her image among the townspeople, but the very *last* person a banker could offend was her largest depositor.

Finally Liz managed to find her voice. "I think you made a mistake here."

She pointed to the figure in question, and Matt leaned forward across the desk until his head almost touched hers. His clean male scent filled her nostrils, and she suddenly felt light-headed.

He returned to the chair. "Do you think I'll need more?"

"*More?*" She cleared her throat. "No, it's fine. It's just that . . ."

Good Lord! She'd almost told him that his was the largest account. He might think the bank couldn't handle it.

"It's fine," she said more firmly. "I'll take care of it right away."

He grinned. "You've got great hands, Liz."

"Thanks," she muttered.

"I'll let you get back to work now." He stood up and thrust out a hand.

She hastily rose to her feet. Although she was reluctant even to touch his hand, she knew she had to. She steeled herself as the warmth he generated now enveloped her fingers and shot like fire up her arm. Someone had great hands, and it wasn't her.

"Don't forget dinner tomorrow night," he said with a pirate's grin.

"I'll bring the wine," she replied in a dull voice.

Might as well, she thought resignedly. She couldn't afford to have him angry with her now; he might pull the account. And the size of it far outweighed any ensuing gossip to the bank's central office.

She might as well get a horse too. Riding naked across the common was looking better and better by the moment.

"Is it true a farmer can get a government subsidy for a one-hundred-thousand-dollar tractor and never have to pay it back?" Matt asked, leaning his elbows on the kitchen table.

Liz chuckled. "I'll bet none of the local farmers told you that."

"Hank Krenshaw, the editor of the *Hopewell Bugle*, told me," Matt replied. "Is it true?"

"I see you're getting around town." Restlessly shifting under his stare, Liz finally nodded. "Yes, it's true. On the surface, at least. But Hank probably didn't bother to add that every local farmer is already in debt for not less than a quarter of a million dollars."

Matt's eyebrows shot up in amazement. "That much?"

"That much. Your average farmer doesn't know the meaning of 'breaking even.' But everyone loves to gossip about everyone else. That's rural life, Matt."

Liz knew she wasn't giving away any bank secrets by telling Matt the realities of farming. While Hopewell was a small town about fifteen miles from the city of Swanton near the Canadian border, its big dairy processing plant made it a gathering place for all the surrounding farms and hamlets. Naturally farm debt, milk production, the weather, and government subsidies were the main topics of local conversation. If people didn't have anything else to talk about.

She smiled, more to herself than to him. The dinner had gone very well, and she even admitted she'd enjoyed herself, although her stomach seemed to drop into a black hole every time Matt had looked at her. And he'd looked at her a lot.

It was his eyes, she decided. Those green eyes darkened whenever they focused on her. In fact, they were darkening right now.

Her smile faltering, she swallowed back a lump of what she hoped wasn't fear. It had been a lovely evening, but it was time to go. Besides, if Matt kept staring at her much longer, she'd probably turn to melted butter.

Pushing back her chair and rising to her feet, she straightened the jacket of her cream-colored suit, then plastered another smile on her face. "I've enjoyed myself, but I don't want to keep you."

Vaguely she waved a hand toward the boxes still lining the wall in the big wood-beamed, brick country kitchen.

Not moving, Matt grinned. "Sit down, Liz. You're forgetting I'm retired now, and I can unpack anytime. Besides, it isn't even nine o'clock yet."

She involuntarily glanced at the clock radio on the counter to confirm his words, then silently cursed her nervous reaction. She didn't intend to allow the early hour to sway her from leaving.

"I do have a few things to do at home before I go to bed . . . sleep." She edged toward the living room. "Thank you for inviting me to dinner. The shish kebab was delicious."

Matt suddenly blocked her path. His hands touched her shoulders. "Liz, why so early? Did I do something wrong?"

"No, no," she assured him breathlessly. "I really can't stay long, Matt."

"But you can stay a little longer. I haven't even shown you through the house yet."

"Okay, but only a little longer," she said, hating herself for being so wishy-washy. One quick tour wouldn't hurt, she thought. But that was it! Matt had been a gracious and gentlemanly host, but she had to be seen leaving his house at an early hour. "I really do have to get home."

"Great."

He removed his hands from her shoulders and tucked her hand in the crook of his elbow to lead her into the living room.

Before dinner she had seen the downstairs

briefly—and noted that Matt was still in the process of unpacking. It was evident that he liked modern paintings, as several cubist prints and strange shapes on canvas were already hanging on the paneled walls.

Staring at a small screaming-yellow and lime-green blob on an enormous white canvas, Liz asked, "What's this supposed to be?"

"What's it look like?" Matt asked in an amused voice.

"Like a chihuahua got sick," she murmured, tilting her head to see if it looked better from another perspective.

Matt roared with laughter, and she grinned, liking the sound of that laugh. Finally he calmed enough to say, "It's supposed to represent man's fight for survival."

"I think man is losing."

Leaving Matt to his second burst of laughter, Liz wandered over to a small unframed painting. She lifted it off the wall to admire it.

"This is a Picasso, isn't it?" she asked, delicately touching the rough surface with a forefinger. "I didn't know they could make a reproduction look and *feel* like the original."

Coming up behind her, Matt answered, "So far as I know, they can't. That's a real Picasso."

With suddenly shaking hands Liz carefully rehung the painting.

"Are all of them originals?" she asked in a small voice as she turned to face him. An original Picasso! And she touched it. He really ought to put signs on them or something.

He was grinning at her nervousness. "No. That's

the only one. Actually, it's not as expensive as you're probably thinking. Picasso was a very prolific painter, and you'd be surprised where and for how little you can find his stuff sometimes. I found this one in a tiny Portuguese tourist shop of all places."

She gave a little gasp of surprise. "You're kidding!"

He shook his head. "Nope. I thought it was just a copy. But a friend who knows art made me take it to an art gallery. The man who appraised it for me said that while I got a bargain, it wasn't done during one of Picasso's best periods. Frankly I wouldn't have cared if it was only worth ten bucks. There's something about a square donkey with four noses that appeals to me."

Liz giggled. She couldn't help it. "He looks elegant. Give or take a nose."

As Matt gazed down at her, a slight smile played across his mobile lips. He was so damn sexy, she thought, with his green eyes and dark beard. And the jeans and pink western shirt he wore casually and yet so confidently made him look even more masculine. She felt her body zing and tighten yet again. Suddenly she couldn't stand the constant flip-flopping inside her any longer.

Frantically she reached up and pulled his head down to hers. Their lips touched, and she forgot her own shocked amazement at what she was doing. Curving his arms around her, Matt instantly took over the kiss, and it was everything she'd unconsciously hoped for. His mouth slanted across hers and dominated it, yet demanded a like response. And she gave it greedily, her tongue swirling with his in an age-old dance. He lifted her on tiptoe and nestled her body tightly against his. His hands stroked their way down her back until they kneaded the soft flesh of her buttocks through her skirt. Then she was pulled even tighter against his hard arousal.

A gentle shock wave rocked her once. It began to grow into a yearning ache, warning her of the explosion that could be with him. Her head spun dizzily. Everything felt so right and so special that she couldn't imagine herself being anywhere else but in his arms. . . .

In his arms?

Three

"Liz?"

Lost in the kiss, it had taken Matt a moment to realize Liz was struggling in his embrace. Involuntarily his arms loosened, and she slipped out of them. Her eyes not meeting his, she straightened her jacket.

"Liz?" he repeated, a puzzled frown crossing his features.

"I'm sorry," she whispered.

"I'm not." He stepped forward, intending to take her in his arms again to find out if the dynamite-packed kiss had been his imagination. He still felt as if he'd been rabbit-punched in the stomach.

Taking a step backward, she straightened and looked directly at him with steady gray eyes. He sensed the effort she was making to retain her control, and it stopped him dead.

"Forget what just happened," she said.

"Not on your life, lady." He couldn't help the grin spreading across his face.

Pink flushed her cheeks, and he wondered if she knew how demure and shy she looked. In three days he'd glimpsed a sex kitten, a trim businesswoman, a witty companion, and a wanton. Such a small package for such a lot of woman. He ignored the sudden urge to reach for her again. She was upset, and he needed to be understanding, not an animal.

He swallowed. It wouldn't be easy.

"Matt, I know what you're thinking"—he wondered if she really did—"but I'm not available."

"What the hell does that mean?"

"It means that I have a good job at the bank, and I don't want to lose it."

Confused, he gave her a blank look. "What's that got to do with us?"

"One kiss does not make an 'us,' " she stated firmly.

"A kiss like that—"

"I'm your banker," she continued, thrusting her chin forward. "And I intend to stay that way. It's the relationship I want, and the only one."

"Could have fooled me," he muttered, eyeing her in frustration.

They stared at each other for a moment, then Liz turned on her heel and marched to the front door. Matt immediately followed, his angry long-legged strides quickly closing the distance. Just as she opened the door he grabbed her left arm none too gently and spun her around.

Realizing he was rapidly losing his temper, he released her and forced himself back in control.

"Look, Liz—"

"Thank you for dinner, Matt," she broke in. "Good night."

He scowled fiercely, but let her slip out the door. Crossing the threshold, he watched her slim figure retreat around the hedge and up her driveway. Her own front door shut with a finality that would have daunted most men.

Matt grinned suddenly. Liz might shut her door, but she had to come out sometime. And he'd be waiting. She was a bundle of feminine contradictions, and he was determined to explore them all.

His sudden and fierce desire for her had surprised him almost as much as her initiating the kiss. He was positive there had been nothing in his life that he'd wanted more than he now wanted Liz. Not even when he'd been a kid desperate to escape the Bronx and had pestered the Ford Modeling Agency until they'd finally given him a job. One kiss. And mixed with the overwhelming need had been an equally strong urge toward protective tenderness.

His burst of laughter broke the still night air. Liz required about as much protection as an enraged tigress. She was smart and independent. And stubborn.

Well, so was he. He'd learned early to go after what he wanted and stick with it until he got it.

He briefly wondered if he was so drawn to her because she was reluctant to acknowledge her attraction to him. Then he dismissed the thought. The kiss proved there was something more there, something not to be ignored. He had no intention of ignoring it.

But Liz had begun drawing battle lines tonight. Given time, she'd enclose herself in them. He couldn't allow that. A little gentle strategy was required, that's all.

"And it better be a good strategy," he muttered aloud.

"I'm retiring after the end of the fiscal year, in September," Joe Malack said, steepling his fingers over his paunch. He gazed around at the large noontime crowd at the Hopewell Inn.

For a long moment Liz stared open-mouthed at her boss, who was seated across the table from her. Even over the din of clinking silverware, clattering dishes, and the calliope of voices, she knew she'd heard him correctly. She just had trouble believing it.

Joe retiring? He was only in his fifties, and considered one of the top banking managers at New England Bank. He oversaw the operations of five branches, of which Liz's branch was one. During her two years at the bank, she and Joe had become good friends. As her superior, he'd never nitpicked over how she ran her branch. Instead, he'd guided her with loose reins and good advice, allowing her to do her job without interference. She'd liked and respected him from their first meeting, and their friendship had grown out of that. Joe treated her more like a favorite niece than his employee, which, in turn, made their business relationship quite relaxed. But she'd never considered that there might be a time when he would leave the bank, and especially not this soon.

"This is a surprise," she finally said, realizing just how much she would miss him.

His gaze returning to her, he nodded. "Jen and I have been talking about it for a while, and we decided we deserved our golden years before we were horizontal."

Liz chuckled.

"Anyway, we've been talking and figuring, and we know we'll be pretty comfortable. Why wait until we're retiring into the old folks home?"

Liz nodded, her mind churning over the other implications of Joe's early retirement. Only two years with the bank, and one as a branch manager, she knew she wouldn't be considered as a candidate to take Joe's place. But it did mean a reshuffling of the branch managers, and she could even move up into the central office in Swanton. It might be a sideways promotion, but she was young, and it could be a good career move for her.

Instantly she felt guilty for even thinking about how Joe's leaving would affect her position within the bank, especially when she didn't want him to retire.

"I'm going to tell Harry Aberman at Central this afternoon," Joe added, breaking into her thoughts. "Just to make it official with the big guys. I thought I'd let you know ahead of time, since I'm recommending you as my replacement."

"Me?" she squeaked.

Joe chuckled. "I thought that would take you by surprise. Yes, you. And not because we're friends, although I feel good about that part of it, but because you're savvy, and you're diplomatic. Small-town Vermonters aren't easy to deal with, yet you've gained their respect this past year. That business with Micah Davis was brilliant."

"But I only made sure he'd be able to pay the loan after that accident with his new bull," Liz protested. "Any bank manager would have done that."

"Very few managers would have persuaded the client to sell his only other prize stud bull *to* the bank to pay off the loan. How's Romeo doing?"

"Excellent," Liz replied. "Micah's clients are up to their hip boots in calves and butterfat."

She remembered how she hadn't wanted her first major decision as Hopewell's new bank manager to be a foreclosure. Micah Davis had a small, unprofitable dairy farm and one superb Holstein breeding bull he'd raised from a calf. That was Romeo. Through artificial insemination dairy farmers improved their stock and made milk production faster, better, and cheaper than by the old-fashioned method. With visions of artificial insemination stud fees whirling in his head, Micah had taken a loan to buy a second mature bull. Unfortunately the bull hadn't liked the threshing machine and challenged it to a fight before anyone could stop it. The bull lost. Micah was left with a $150,000 debt and no bull to pay it off. He'd needed a good deal of persuasion to sell Romeo, the darling of his herd, to the bank. But he had finally caved in when Liz had guaranteed, in writing, that he'd manage the bull for the bank for a share of the stud fees. The bank was not allowed to sell Romeo for five years, and then Micah had first chance to purchase the bull back. Romeo had always lived up to his name, and everyone was pleased with the deal. Especially Romeo; now he had even more ladies to love. Indirectly, of course.

"I doubt anyone would have come up with such a creative and profitable solution," Joe said, laughing. "If you had foreclosed, Micah would have lost his Romeo at the least of it, and I doubt we really would have made more than legal fees. You've proven yourself here in Hopewell, Liz, and I wanted you to know you were getting my recommendation for district manager."

"But—"

Joe held up a hand to stop her words. "Liz, don't worry about what your ex-husband did. It had no bearing on our hiring you in the first place, and it will have no bearing on a promotion for you. The authorities in Chicago were very satisfied that you were never involved in it, and even praised you for giving them full cooperation at the time. You're the best person for the district manager job. And that's the bottom line, Liz."

She stared down at her plate. Wonderful, "go-getter" Jonathan Mansfield, she thought bitterly. Executive extraordinaire—and immoral thief. Shortly after their marriage, she'd discovered her corporate vice-president husband fully expected her to embezzle funds and to implement other questionable "irregularities" in her position as assistant manager at a Chicago bank. It hadn't taken her more than five minutes to pack her bags and file for a divorce, feeling like the worst fool. Jonathan had had better luck, though, seducing a female loan officer at another bank into his schemes . . . until they'd been caught. Unfortunately that had happened just two weeks before the divorce became final. The ensuing humiliation had been almost unbearable for Liz. She'd found out much later that her superiors had quietly audited her bank to see if she'd also "cooperated" with Jonathan. While she'd been completely cleared, she knew her career there had ground to a screeching halt. She'd applied to financial institutions across the country, and when New England offered, she had grabbed the job. New England Bank had been good to her, and good for her self-respect. But Jonathan's dirty stain had not totally disappeared. She wondered if it ever would.

"Thank you." She didn't know what else to say to Joe for his confidence in her, and the opportunity he was extending. But she nearly fell off her chair at his next words.

"Your coup in getting this Matt Callahan account couldn't have come at a more opportune time."

"I . . . ah . . ." She felt the heat rising up her throat as she remembered their kiss. Ruthlessly she forced down the blush. "I can't take credit for that, Joe. He just walked into the bank and signed up."

"Well, it looks very good just now. He's a neighbor of yours, isn't he?"

"Just moved in this week," she answered promptly. Obviously Joe had read the application forms to know Matt was a neighbor. He'd also know the "single" box had been checked. "I barely know him."

Joe eyed her with speculation, then said, "He called me yesterday."

"What!"

"Said he was very pleased with the friendly treatment he'd received at the bank. You look shocked."

Liz realized she was gaping at him. She composed herself and said, "Just surprised he'd call, I guess. I'll have to thank him next time I see him."

That dirty, rotten . . . Furious, she couldn't conjure up a word unprintable enough to call Matt. She was positive he'd done it to let her know she had to be beholden to him as a depositor. If it wasn't for the possibility of a promotion, she'd tell Matt where to stuff his account.

Liz plastered a pleased smile on her face. "Thank you, Joe, for your recommendation and your faith in my abilities. I really appreciate it, knowing others have more seniority with New England. If Central does take your recommendation, I promise I won't let you down."

"I never thought you would." Joe grinned. "I expect you'll handle Callahan with your usual diplomacy and tact."

Liz nodded, thinking she'd rather let Romeo handle Matt. Romeo's usual form of diplomacy was a mixture of mean disposition and twelve-inch razor-sharp horns.

"No. I don't want in, Mike," Matt said as he opened his front door in answer to whoever was persistently knocking on it. Grinning at the sight of Liz standing on his threshold, he cradled the telephone receiver against his shoulder and waved her inside. "That bill could get killed in the committee sessions at any moment. Support for offshore drilling in that state is only marginal. You know that."

"The governor is supporting it, and that will make a big difference. This is a real ground-floor opportunity . . ."

Mike's words faded as Matt watched Liz march into his living room, her straight back radiating fury. He smiled to himself. She was so fragile-looking, like a porcelain figurine, but she packed a hidden wallop. He had the distinct feeling she was about to wallop him. It looked like his first move to draw her out was working.

"Not interested. Good-bye, Mike," Matt said into the telephone.

"But . . ."

"Good-bye."

He hung up the phone. Some investment groups never took no for an answer.

"Hi, Liz," he said softly as he closed the door. He walked over to where she was standing by the sofa. Other than a brief glimpse of her going and coming from the bank, this was the first he'd seen of her in the three days since the dinner. She really ought to get out more often.

"Why is your car in *my* driveway?" she asked.

"Trees."

Confusion instantly took the place of the angry expression on her face. "Did you say trees?"

"Mmmm." Matt studied the way her smooth shining hair just touched her slim shoulders. His gaze drifted farther down to the tailored lines of her khaki suit. The jacket hid the curve of her breasts, but the skirt hinted at the beautifully rounded thighs underneath.

She looked good in his living room. Damn good. His modern paintings seemed to match her changing moods, the hard woods of the desk and tables her stubborn core, and the muted tones of the blue plush sofa expressed her softness. It was almost as if he'd put the room together for her.

A finger rudely poked him in the chest, bringing back his wandering attention.

"What the hell do trees have to do with your car being in my driveway?" she asked, her voice laced with acid.

He shrugged. "I black-topped my driveway today. How about staying for dinner? I'll whip up something good."

"You're about to 'whip up' my patience, Matthew Callahan. Get your car out of my driveway. *Now!*"

He shrugged again, but was silently pleased. She was reacting to him with sparks and fire. Unfortunately he had had to light the wrong end of the firecracker to get them. Well, at least the fireworks were started.

"You're blowing this all out of proportion, Liz. I borrowed your driveway only for a little while. I know it was presumptuous of me, but I didn't want to leave the 'Vette at the curb. Not with all these trees. The tree sap and the birds would ruin the finish. As a banker, you can understand the importance of upkeep on a property."

He could see her visibly rein in her temper. She took a noticeable breath and smiled sweetly at him, satisfaction lighting her eyes. Matt suddenly felt as if he'd just walked into a trap.

"Surely, as a bank customer, you can realize

the importance of your banker's reputation, Matt. How does it look with your car in my driveway, no matter how innocent the reason?"

"But you weren't home, and—"

"Doesn't matter. It *looks* as if we're more than neighbors."

"Come on, Liz. That kind of thing went out with poodle skirts and D.A.'s. This is the eighties. Nobody cares what two adults are doing."

Liz threw up her hands in exasperation. "And this isn't New York. Hopewell has a grapevine that moves faster than the speed of light. That phone call you just had will be all over town before dinnertime."

"What!"

She gave a wicked laugh, obviously enjoying his consternation. "The phone company must have told you you're on a temporary party line."

He frowned in confusion. The telephone installer had mentioned it yesterday when he'd connected the phone line. He'd claimed it was because of the town's small size that the telephone company didn't bother with installing private lines until they had to.

"Yes, but . . ."

"People listen in. In fact, several of the towns-people keep a party line because they love to listen in. Hopewell may not have poodle skirts and the ducks' rears may be on real ducks, but that old-time mentality is still there."

"Dammit!" Matt burst out, beginning to pace the room furiously. "I can't be on a damn party line! My business depends on secrecy!"

"Business?" Liz repeated, grabbing his arm as

he passed by her. He stopped and faced her. "What business? Did you falsify the bank records? I swear I really will let Romeo loose on you."

"Who's Romeo?" Matt shouted, forgetting about his problems with the party line. He didn't even want to consider *why* she'd call a man Romeo.

"A very mean bull. What business, Matt?"

"My investments. Romeo had better be a real bull."

"Four hooves, swishing tail, and razor-sharp horns," Liz replied. She rubbed a hand across her forehead. "I think we're getting off the track here. Just move your car out of my driveway, okay? And don't put it back there again. Oh! Do me a favor and don't mow my lawn either. Now that you know the facts, I think you can understand why."

Matt felt as if he'd been putting together an atom bomb and it had backfired. In his enthusiasm to get together with Liz, he'd never realized how it could come across to observers. Evidently Hopewell had a real network of them. Liz's recent standoffishness wasn't internal, but had to do with her very valid concern for maintaining her reputation. No wonder she was so furious to find his car in her driveway. And mowing her lawn had added to the damage. Being nice and neighborly wasn't turning out exactly as Matt had planned.

But what someone might think didn't change what he was beginning to feel for Liz. There had to be a way around causing any gossip. Unfortunately it was obvious she wasn't about to help him.

Matt groaned to himself. He had a feeling a twenty-hour modeling shoot in the heat and stench of Tunisia would be easier on the nerves than winning Liz. Then again, if one fought for something, it always had greater value.

"Matt, please go move your car," Liz said, breaking into his thoughts.

"In a minute. I want to ask you something." He stared down at her, wondering exactly how to phrase this. "If we lived somewhere less 'civilized,' would you consider mixing business with pleasure?"

"I never mix business with pleasure. It's bad practice."

He almost believed her, until he saw her gaze shift away from his for an instant.

"Liar," he said softly.

"I am not lying," she protested stiffly, her shoulders straightening.

"In this case you are."

With one arm he snagged her around the waist and pulled her against him. Despite her petiteness, they fit together perfectly. She was so tiny and so soft. Ignoring her startled exclamation, he bent and fit his mouth to hers, then probed into the sweetness beyond.

At first Liz didn't respond, but he coaxed her tongue with his own. Suddenly he felt a deep satisfaction as she surrendered to the kiss. Lord, but she felt good, tasted good. And she wanted him. His satisfaction and his yearning doubled at the thought.

He slipped his hand inside her jacket and cupped her breast, feeling the nipple come alive at his touch. She gave a tiny moan in the back of her throat, pressing even closer against him and curving her arms around his neck. Her breast seemed to grow in his hand, and his fingers delighted in its weight. Her long nails clawed his shoulders, and all the blood in his body instantly poured into his loins.

Matt tore his lips away from her mouth and buried them in the softness of her throat. He ran his hands up and down the sides of her body before letting them sink into the flesh of her derriere. He knew she would be soft everywhere, and he wanted to test himself against that softness, feel it surrounding him like a satin prison.

"You drive a man insane," he murmured against her ear. "I promise I'll be more discreet from now on."

Suddenly he was embracing air. Again.

Immediately straightening, he glared at her. "Dammit, Liz! You do that every time we're kissing. Are you allergic to kisses, or what?"

Liz straightened her clothes before lifting her head. Her cheeks were flushed to a delicate rose, and her gray eyes were still bright with passion.

"To yours, evidently," she replied flatly.

He eyed her for a moment, resisting the temptation to paddle her beautiful bottom. "Shall we test that allergy theory?"

"No, thank you. Please remove your car from my drive."

"Next you'll be telling me the attraction we feel for each other is all in my head," he said between clenched teeth.

Her chin rose defiantly. "I don't intend to fall

into bed with you because of a simple sexual attraction. Instant gratification is meaningless."

He gave her a look of disbelief. "If you think this is a simple attraction, you've got a lot to learn about men and women, sweetheart."

"Open your ears and—"

"My ears are open. But your body said a lot more. You want what I want; you're just worried about what someone else might say. They'll say it anyway, no matter what we do."

"And we'll do nothing," Liz replied angrily.

"We'll do everything, Elizabeth O'Neal. You can try to fight it all you want, but I'm not a quitter. Eventually I'll win. But I promise not to hurt your image as a proper banker in the process. Now I'll go move my car." He turned on his heel and stalked out of the house.

The damn driveway ought to be dry by now anyway.

Four

"Car trouble, Liz?"

"Hello, Emily," Liz said, halting her brisk strides down Elm Street, four short blocks from her home on Rodgers Street.

She smiled politely at the big raw-boned woman who was sweeping the sidewalk in front of her house, but wasn't fooled by the friendly smile the older woman returned. Emily Richards swam the gossip waters with sharklike enthusiasm, and Liz knew she'd have a bite taken out of her if she weren't careful. Why hadn't she walked down Markham Road to the common instead of cutting across Elm? Then she could have avoided most of the town's residences. She unconsciously tightened her grip on her soft oxblood briefcase.

"No car trouble," she went on. "It's a beautiful day, so I thought I'd walk to the bank."

Emily glanced up at the bright sky. "Ayuh. It's a good day for walking. Hear tell that new neighbor of yours is a real gardener. He bought eight rose bushes from Stanley's Garden Supply yesterday, and twenty pounds of fertilizer. No grass seed though. Is he gonna wait till fall to seed his place?"

Liz forced down a caustic reply. Instead, she shrugged. "I don't know, Emily."

"Figured you might, havin' dinner with him and all."

"Mr. Callahan wanted to discuss some important banking business," she said, gritting her teeth against her rising anger. She knew this would happen. "I thought it was very nice of him to ask me to dinner, when we'd barely said hello. After all, he's *very* busy moving in."

"Guess so. Always takes a lot to get settled in a house."

In spite of her anger, Liz managed to keep a straight face at Emily's remark. The woman still lived in the same house she'd been born in over fifty years ago.

"A new house is a good deal of work. Well, I better be getting on to the bank—"

"Marla Givens told me he's paying the telephone company extra to get him on a private line. They're coming out today to put it in." Emily laughed. "Marla's madder than a wet hen. Says she coulda gotten rich from his phone calls. He's some sort of fancy stockbroker, ain't he?"

"Why don't you ask him," Liz suggested with a syrupy tone. She silently acknowledged she couldn't edge around Emily and continue on her way without being impolite. Besides, there was nothing left to edge around; the woman's bulk took up the width of the sidewalk.

"He doesn't say much about himself," Emily went on, " 'cept he's retired. Kind of a mystery man." She pulled a piece of paper from her apron pocket and unfolded it. She held it out to Liz. "Wondered, though, if this could be him."

Her heart dropping, Liz stared at the magazine ad Emily had shoved under her nose. The beard was nonexistent, but the male model posing in the black bikini briefs was definitely Matt. There was no mistaking his green eyes and wicked smile in the full-color layout. Her gaze roved over the slick page, searching out the little things she knew about Matt's physique. She found the lock of his hair that always insisted on dipping forward over his forehead, the slight quirk in the left eyebrow, the fine-boned yet strong hands. She also found the hard planes of his chest and thighs that had fitted themselves so tightly to her own.

"There is some resemblance," she finally replied in a faint voice. She cleared her throat. "But I really don't know if it's Matt or not."

Still gazing at the ad, she didn't notice the sharp look Emily gave her when she used Matt's first name. She blinked in confusion, though, as Emily carefully refolded the paper and slipped it back into her apron pocket.

"Just curious if you knew he liked to pose near naked for everyone to see."

Liz gaped for a moment at the woman's audacity. How was she supposed to know about Matt's past, especially a near naked one? Suddenly she was furious. Didn't anyone in Hopewell have anything better to do than gossip?

"Modeling is a respected business, Emily, and

a profitable one. Whoever the model is for that ad, he has to be extremely good at his craft. Now, if you'll excuse me, the bank doesn't open until I'm there."

Her briefcase banging against her knee, Liz marched onto the grass at the curb, around Emily, and back onto the sidewalk. Her strides ate up the concrete at a furious pace until she turned the corner onto Willow Street. Once out of Emily's sight, she leaned weakly against a tree and, with shaking hands, pulled a pack of cigarettes and a lighter from her briefcase. She quickly lit a cigarette and blew out a soothing curl of smoke.

"Old battle-ax," she muttered. "At least she didn't know about his car being in the driveway."

Liz grimaced at her overly optimistic words. Emily probably knew all about it. She just hadn't had a chance to bring the topic into the conversation. Damn Matt! This was all his fault in the first place. Why couldn't he have been a real city person and just ignored his neighbor? Instead, he was the most infuriating man she'd ever met.

Straightening away from the tree and beginning to walk toward the bank again, she took a second puff of the cigarette . . . and then realized it was her *third* one of the day.

"Dammit!"

Walking to the curb, she tossed the cigarette into the street and ground it out beneath a high-heeled pump. She returned to the sidewalk, cursing under her breath as she continued walking. If she wasn't breaking cigarettes over Matt, she was smoking more than her self-imposed quota. Yesterday she'd smoked half a pack of the filthy things, and no matter how much she'd lectured herself for back-sliding, she hadn't been able to stop.

It was the waiting.

And that was Matt's fault too. It had been almost a full week since their argument. Six days since he'd declared they'd do "everything." So far, they'd barely nodded to each other in passing. Otherwise, Matt ignored her.

Liz wasn't sure whether she was grateful or disappointed. She knew only she was sick of being on Matt's seesaw. She wanted off, and she wanted off now.

Glaring at the sidewalk, she perversely wondered if he'd decided not to bother with her. Maybe he'd realized it was only a simple physical attraction after all. Maybe her bitchy attitude had turned him off.

"Maybe you'd better stop thinking about it, girl," she scolded herself aloud. "The only seesaw you're on is one you made yourself."

Joe Malack had gone out on a limb for her by recommending her for his job after his retirement. He wouldn't have done it if he hadn't had confidence in her abilities to handle every aspect of the job. And that meant keeping Matt at a distance.

It certainly looked as if she'd achieved that objective.

Liz forced away a sudden wave of vague disappointment and instead acknowledged she was being foolish even to speculate on why Matt wasn't interested in her any longer. She should be happy he wasn't. She *was* happy he wasn't, she firmly told herself. She'd only bruised his libido, and that was why he'd spouted those typical male threats. In fact, if she hadn't been so overwhelmed by him in the beginning, he probably would have exhibited only a passing interest in her. If he'd had any interest at all in her as more than a neighbor. But she had been the one to kiss first. . . .

Liz touched her lips with a finger, then dropped her hand to her side and mentally shook herself for remembering something better left forgotten.

As she'd told him: One kiss does not a relationship make. And it didn't. Everything was back to normal now, at least. Matt was just another Hopewell resident, her image would survive a few minor sideswipes, and she had even been recommended for a promotion. No one had ever supported her as Joe had, not even her parents. And she vowed not to let him down.

A frown touching her brow, she decided life was just peachy keen again. She only wished she felt peachy keen too.

She pushed aside her disturbing thoughts and was mildly surprised to discover herself at the bank's back door. She chuckled dryly and fished in her briefcase for her keys, knowing she must have walked the rest of the way by rote. Maybe there were such things as guardian angels.

"But, Matt, corn futures are at an all-time low right now. I think you should buy."

"I don't know," Matt slowly replied into the telephone receiver and leaned back against the sofa. Barry Stevens, his broker, was really pushing for an investment, but other factors indicated a possible poor risk in corn futures. "It would be tempting, except for the advance weather forecasts. They're predicting a hot summer for the Midwest. If it is, the corn will love it, and bushel prices will drop even more from oversupply."

"Okay, Matt. I just thought I'd let all my clients know corn futures are looking very good . . . but you're the one with the money."

Matt grinned at Barry's "you'll be sorry" tone. He knew better than to trust it. Barry had had the same attitude on orange juice futures, until a mild winter caused an overabundance of oranges and rock-bottom prices on the market. A careful buyer was always aware his broker could be wrong on occasion. And Matt considered himself a very careful buyer.

Propping his feet on the glass coffee table, he said, "I've been talking to some old friends, and they tell me mohair is coming back into fashion this winter. The price is pretty low right now. . . ."

"How many shares do you want?" Barry asked excitedly.

Matt gave a short laugh and named a figure. Barry rushed him off the phone, and as he hung up Matt knew corn futures were about to give way to mohair futures. Mohair was definitely a better investment at this point anyway.

"Well, one thing's going right," he muttered, frowning slightly. He patted the phone before shifting it off his lap. "And one problem solved."

He'd had to pay the telephone company a huge fee to have a private line installed, but it had been worth it. Now he didn't have to worry about being overheard by anyone. Thank heavens Liz had told him about eavesdroppers.

Liz.

Matt groaned, finally admitting he had no idea how to go about winning Liz short of breaking down her door and carrying her off to a secluded spot to make love. While the idea was very satisfying, the method was hardly discreet. But after days of almost no contact, he was desperate.

If only he hadn't made it sound like a game he would win. Then he might have been able to salvage something of a friendship with her and build from there. Liz was a deadly serious business to him, yet he'd made her sound like the kewpie doll prize at a shooting gallery. Winner take all. No wonder she wasn't speaking to him.

He was using excuses, and he knew it. Sure, he could blame himself for sounding heavy-handed and macho, and he had. But Liz was also using excuses for not acknowledging the spark of attraction between them. They were equally to blame for the present stalemate.

Matt chuckled. At least they had some kind of equality between them. He'd always thought of women as his equal, and was now thinking of Liz as a very special equal partner. But she seemed beyond his reach at the moment. After seeing a few townspeople in action, he couldn't help but admit she was right on the subject of discretion. In three trips to the common, where the bank and the shops were located, he'd been told by several local males about Stanley Gruber's love affair with the whiskey bottle, Marla Givens's hidden library of Harold Robbins novels, and that Bert Cuthbert cheated on his wife whenever he went into Swanton. It boggled his mind to consider what he might hear on his next trip.

Matt shuddered at the thought of putting Liz and himself under Hopewell's microscope. Somehow, though, he'd find a circumspect way to pursue her. Her resistance was only as strong as her desire to maintain her image as an upstanding citizen. She'd practically admitted that herself. All he had to do was pull a trick rabbit out of his hat, and she'd crumble.

Maybe.

Scowling, Matt told himself not to be stupid. Liz had already physically expressed her feelings. She'd all but pulled him inside out when she had! The problem, though, was finding that damn rabbit.

Hours later Matt grinned broadly as he watched the late night movie. On the screen Errol Flynn, as Don Juan, glanced around a fake seventeenth-century garden before climbing over the balcony of his latest conquest. So far the guy had all the women wondering who would be the next lucky lady to receive his attentions.

If it was good enough for Don Juan, then it was good enough for him.

Matt shoved himself off the sofa and hurried over to the side window that faced Liz's house. Pushing aside the heavy cream-colored curtains, he gazed across the yard. Her lights were out. She must be in bed, and if she weren't asleep yet, she soon would be.

"Perfect," Matt said.

* * *

In the deep shadows of the night Matt approached Liz's back door. Dressed completely in black to camouflage himself against prying eyes, he grasped the doorknob with a gloved hand and tested it. The door was locked, but there was only one lock and it was an old one. Piece of cake.

He slid a credit card from the back pocket of his jeans and began wiggling it between the doorjamb and the door while jiggling the door handle. The door wouldn't budge.

"Open sesame, dammit," he cursed in a bare whisper.

Continuing to wiggle and jiggle, he could feel beads of perspiration already forming on his forehead. This always worked in the movies, he thought. He pressed the credit card harder into the narrow gap.

The door opened suddenly with a loud click.

For an instant he stared at it, shocked that the lock had actually given. Then he slipped inside and let his eyes adjust to the darker shapes of the kitchen. The table and chairs were against the window to his left, leaving a clear path into the next room. He tucked the card back into his pocket.

"Don't leave home without it," he said with a quiet chuckle.

Moving swiftly and quietly through the house and up the stairs, he listened carefully for any noise that indicated Liz might have awakened. He heard nothing.

On the second floor he headed straight for the

third door on the right, knowing that room was the master bedroom. He'd wistfully observed those lights going out at eleven-thirty every night, until he'd felt like a fantasizing schoolboy. This, though, was a much better fantasy, he decided.

At the door of Liz's bedroom he stopped and leaned one arm on the jamb. A slow smile touched his lips as he gazed longingly at the slender form outlined under the bedclothes. Then he walked to the double bed, his sneakers soundless on the plush carpet. Liz was sleeping on her side, facing him. Her hands were tucked under her chin, and her hair was a pale, tousled halo surrounding her delicate features.

She could almost be a child, Matt thought as an odd tenderness washed over him. But the curve of her derriere was all woman, and the sight of it provoked a very male response. It tempted him to forget his good intentions and join her in the double bed, but with a struggle he finally forced the thought away.

For a lingering moment more he savored Liz's peaceful face. Then, pulling a single red rose out of the waistband of his jeans, Matt laid it near the outer edge of the second pillow. Giving in to one small temptation, he braced his hand on the old-fashioned maple bedpost and leaned farther over the bed.

The touch of his lips was feather-light on her brow.

Smiling down at her, he straightened. As he crept out of the room he decided he could have given lessons on romance to Errol Flynn.

Hell, he could have given lessons to Don Juan too.

Five

Liz's sleep was penetrated by a familiar and annoying buzzing. Her fogged brain automatically commanded a hand to stretch across the pillow to shut off the noise. But then that hand encountered something she knew shouldn't be there. Something sticklike and hard attached to a velvety-soft ball. With a monumental effort she opened one eye.

There was a rose on her pillow.

For a long moment Liz gazed at it, wondering why she had brought a rose to bed with her. It really was the oddest thing to do, she told herself sleepily and rolled over onto her back.

Suddenly her second eyelid snapped open, and she shot up into a sitting position. Whipping her head to her left, she stared in disbelief at the red rose lying in solitary splendor on her pillow.

"Ohmigod," she whispered in a hoarse voice as shivers of terror ran down her spine. Some perverted nut had broken into her house during the night, watched her sleeping, and left a rose on her pillow. Someone in nice little Hopewell had to be crazy. Some insane . . .

She suddenly realized *who* in Hopewell was crazy. And that—that maniac lived right next door to her. But Matt Callahan wasn't crazy at all. He was showing her how easy it was to be in her bed. And how she'd spread her own petals and bloom under his touch, just like the rose. That damn rose didn't mean anything more than her expected, unconditional surrender to him.

A red haze of fury clouding her vision, Liz snatched up the rose and scrambled off the bed. She stopped only to throw on her blue terry robe before racing down the stairs and unlocking the front door.

"I'll show him that he can't play mind games with me," she muttered, clutching the rose in her right hand like a baseball bat. "Break into my house . . . leave a rose like some stud lover . . . see me asleep. See me asleep? That lowlife watched me sleep! The hell with showing him, I'll kill him!"

She slammed the door behind her, marched across the adjoining lawns, and up the steps of Matt's porch. She banged her fist against the brightly painted red door, shattering the early morning quiet. When the door didn't open instantly, she banged on it again. And kept banging.

The door finally swung open, and a dark-velour-robed Matt stood glaring at her, like a harsh and omnipotent god, the impact of his presence momentarily overwhelming. Then his green eyes softened and his big body relaxed.

"Liz!" he exclaimed before she could speak. He reached out and quickly pulled her inside. "I'm so glad you've finally decided to give up this farce. But this is hardly discreet, honey. It looks like I'll have to arrange our meetings from now on."

He shut the door, and it was another shocking moment before Liz finally found her voice. More angry than ever, she slashed the air in front of him with the rose. "What the hell do you think this is, Matt Callahan?"

He tilted his head to examine the flower. "It looks like a rose."

"Damn right, it's a rose!" she shouted.

"Do I go to the head of the class? Or do I have to guess what variety it is first?"

"You can tell me how it got on my pillow last night."

"On your pillow?" he asked in a voice that sounded genuinely surprised.

Liz took a deep breath and firmly told herself not to lose her temper. It didn't work, and she swatted him with the rose. "You broke into my house last night, came into my bedroom, and left the rose on my pillow. You watched me sleep!"

"If you were sleeping, how do you know it was me?" Matt asked logically.

"Because you're the only qualified pervert in Hopewell!"

He grinned. "Nice to know you think so highly of me, Liz. Actually the rose sounds more like the work of a secret admirer. As you know, I'm an open one." He paused and thoughtfully rubbed his beard. "I don't like having competition, though. Let alone one so suave and gallant as to leave a rose on your pillow."

Liz uttered a barnyard curse. If he ever set foot in her house again, she'd shoot him, she decided.

"Shocking language for a banker," Matt commented. "I wonder if your secret admirer knows you've got a mouth that would make a sailor blush. Personally, I think it shows you've got a good deal of passion. Besides, I curse when I'm angry, so why shouldn't you? It just proves we've got passionate natures, although we already know that, don't we?"

She swallowed back the second curse on her lips, vowing not to give him the satisfaction of hearing it. Matt was deliberately trying to provoke her anger even further, and she'd fallen right into his trap. The thought was enough to cool her anger into a cold lump of ashes. He was obviously aware her emotions were always out of balance whenever she was around him, and he was using them against her. He was a very shrewd game player, but she didn't have the inclination to play.

Cool air drifting across her bare ankles made Liz aware of another, much more intimate fact. They were both dressed only in bathrobes. At least she was wearing the additional but flimsy protection of a nightgown. She had the feeling, though, that Matt's robe was the only thing between her and his total exposure. She hoped not, but a helpless downward glance told her Matt's feet were as bare as hers. Several inches of male legs showed between the hem of his robe and the floor, and the deep V of the robe's collar revealed a wide band of silky hair and hard chest.

One quick flick of the belt, and Matt would be as naked as the day he was born.

Her body heat rising alarmingly, Liz had the sudden urge to untie that belt. She swallowed and forced herself to stand very still. She willed Matt to stand very still too. One move, and she was a goner.

"So," he said, crossing his arms over his chest, "since we've established I'm no 'secret admirer,' what are you going to do about the guy?"

Liz silently sent thanks heavenward that his one move hadn't been toward her. But she couldn't give away her inner turmoil with some wimpy answer or he'd take advantage of that too.

She smiled, hoping it looked sickly sweet and not just sickly. "You really want to know?"

He nodded, his eyes narrowing slightly. Evidently her smile was sickly sweet. She wanted to let her breath out in a whoosh, but resisted.

"First of all, I'm going to call the police and report an escaped psycho . . ."

"Bad move, Liz. Think of all the gossip it will create when the cop cars pull up in front of your house."

"My goodness, Matt, you really have my best interests at heart." Sometimes game-playing was in order, Liz decided. "The cops are out. Maybe I should borrow Romeo for a few days and let him pasture in my yard. One ton of mean bull ought to be enough to scare anyone off."

"That does have merit. But how do you explain Romeo to the neighbors?"

"I'm going into the dairy business."

"Bulls don't give milk."

"Good point." She made a show of tapping her chin in concentration, then shrugged. "Well, I'm sure I can think up some little surprise. I'm sorry I mistook you for my admirer. I really don't know how I could have. You're nowhere near as suave and gallant as he is. Have a nice day, Matt."

Feeling she'd had the last word, and a very effective one, Liz turned on her heel and opened the front door . . . and immediately shut it on the sight of Corey Wilson across the street delivering newspapers. She collapsed against the door and closed her eyes in embarrassment.

"Forget something?" Matt asked in an amused voice.

"Only my brains," she muttered. She straightened away from the door and turn back to him, lifting her chin to a dignified angle. "Matt, I always seem to make an idiot of myself around you, don't I?"

"Forget it. I've done my share with you." He chuckled, moving beside her. "Now, who's out there?"

"Corey, with the morning papers."

"No problem. He'll be gone in a moment."

He silently waited with her until there was an audible *thunk* on the porch. Matt motioned her back away from the door.

"I'll check the street."

Liz didn't breathe as Matt opened the door and stepped outside. With straining ears she heard him pad across the porch. There was more silence, and she knew he was checking the surrounding houses for activity. Maybe her luck would be good and—

Suddenly she realized that no matter how fast she could possibly run, anyone could pick that moment to look out of a window and see her. In her nightgown and robe she was well and truly stuck. There was no logical way to explain her leaving his house at seven in the morning. Even if she suddenly grew wings, she still couldn't fly over the rooftops. That would attract even more attention.

Feeling helpless and depressed, Liz turned away from the open door and dragged herself over to the stairs. Sitting down on the third step from the bottom, she propped her chin in her hands. Realizing she was still holding the rose, she absently stuffed it into her pocket while contemplating the fates.

"Dammit, Liz! What the hell are you doing sitting on the steps?" Matt asked impatiently as he strode into the house. "You should be over here, ready to go—"

"I'm sitting on the steps, wishing I had paid more attention in my chemistry classes," Liz interrupted, slowly rising to her feet.

"Chemistry!"

"Maybe then I'd know the formula for making myself invisible. That's the only way I'll get out of here."

Matt scowled at her. "Don't be ridiculous. It'll take only two seconds to run across the lawns. Nobody will see you."

"Matt, anyone can look outside during those two seconds," she said, shaking her head. "And

they'll see their upstanding bank manager running for her life with her bathrobe hiked up to
her knees. I just can't take the chance of going
out your front door."

Gazing into her distressed gray eyes, Matt silently and thoroughly cursed himself for putting
her in this predicament. Granted, he hadn't expected her to show up on his doorstep before
breakfast, but the responsibility for getting her
back to her house unseen was his.

Feeling that increasingly familiar protectiveness
rise up inside him, he walked over to her and put
his arms around her in comfort. She didn't return his embrace, but she didn't resist either.

"I'm sorry, Liz. If only Corey hadn't already been
around with the papers, we could have disguised
you as him. Can you call in sick at the bank?
Then you could stay here all day. . . ."

She stiffened and pulled away. "No. Anyway, I
have to be there today. It's important."

"Okay," he replied, sensing she couldn't be
swayed. "Maybe some coffee will help us—"

He cut off his own words as an idea popped into
his head. Ignoring her puzzled frown, he worked
through the details. It was crazy, but it might just
work.

"Liz, could you stand a little claustrophobia? If
you can, I think I can get you out of here."

"I suppose." Shaking her head again, she chuckled wryly. "Actually, I'd do anything."

He grinned at her. "Anything?"

Her face flushed, and she nervously rubbed her
forehead. "Matt, I really hate repeating myself . . ."

The smile dropped from his face. "Forget it,

honey. I already got the message. You might as well make yourself some coffee while I get things ready, okay?"

She nodded. "Is there anything else I can do?"

"Just practice being the trash."

"I can't believe I'm going to do this!" Liz said with a groan twenty minutes later.

"Well, if you can think of a better way to get out of here without being seen, go ahead," Matt said, grinning. He was dressed in cutoff jeans and a sweatshirt, its sleeves ripped out.

Hands on her hips, Liz kept her gaze on the large packing carton she was to hide in. She knew Matt had reinforced the bottom so she wouldn't fall out of it, and he'd already cut a small hole in the hedge out by the gardening shed. One side of the carton had been cut, also, and was held together only with packing tape.

"You're going to carry me out to the backyard in this carton like I'm the trash, and then I'm supposed to climb through the hedge and pretend I'm out by the shed to smoke a cigarette?" she asked in awe.

It sounded ridiculous, she thought, but she couldn't help believing it would work. Somehow, crazy things always did. At least no one would see her until she "magically" appeared at the shed. She only hoped any observer would be questioning his eyesight and not how she got there in the first place. And Matt would bring out several more boxes and place them with the first, as if he were getting them out of his way before they went in the trash.

"The plan's foolproof, and you're always smoking by the shed," he pointed out. "By the way, lately you've been out there more than three times."

"I had a setback." She wasn't about to tell him he was the setback.

"There is another way to quit. . . ."

"I saw *Cold Turkey* and forget it! Sex doesn't cure everything," Liz replied caustically. There was a long silence, and she glanced up into Matt's amused eyes. "Don't say it! Don't even think of saying it!"

He laughed. "Just get in the box, and I won't."

She immediately stepped over the edge and sat down. She stood back up.

"Wait a minute. You'll hurt yourself if you try to pick this up from the floor." She glanced around the garage and spotted a small workbench. "The box would be easier to lift from on top of the bench."

"Why, Liz, I didn't know you cared," Matt exclaimed, and planted a smacking kiss on her lips.

She felt the sudden rush of blood to her face. "Dammit, Matt!"

He suddenly swung her up into his arms and set her down feetfirst on the floor.

"I could carry you anywhere, but I think you're probably right about it being easier to lift the carton from up there." He grinned. "I wouldn't want you all upset about my hurting myself."

Still flushed, Liz glared at him as he picked up the empty box and placed it on the workbench. She refused to admit she'd been concerned about *him.* She would have felt the same about anyone lifting a heavy object from the ground.

He turned around and crooked a finger at her. With a last grumble of frustration she climbed up on the wooden stool in front of the workbench. She hesitated for a moment, the sides seeming higher than when the box had been on the ground.

"Here," Matt said, putting his hands around her waist to steady her. She'd just opened her mouth to object when he added, "I'll brace myself against the side, so it won't fall off."

She glanced down in confusion, then realized the edge of the carton overlapped the bench about two or three inches. Maybe this wasn't such a good idea, she thought, but decided to get into the box anyway. Matt would probably turn a protest from her into another innuendo.

With his help she swung one leg, then the other, over the top of the carton. She crouched down.

He flipped the ends closed over her head and said, "All set. You know, Liz, I like having you worry about me, but I promise I won't hurt myself. I wouldn't dare. You may still need me for that cigarette cure."

Huddled down in the darkness, Liz banged on the side of the carton. "Shut up and start playing trashman!"

She squirmed around trying to find a comfortable position in which to brace herself and yet spread her weight evenly along the edges. The only one that even remotely worked was on her hands and knees, like a dog. She heard the click and whirr of the automatic garage door opener.

"Ready?" Matt asked.

"No, but go ahead."

She could feel the pressure of his arms as they curved around the carton. There was a rocking motion and a sudden heave, and she found herself helplessly jolted against all four sides at once.

"Stop bouncing around like that, or you'll fall out," Matt warned, his voice muffled by the cardboard.

"Stop bouncing me around like that, and I won't," she half-shouted, finding it impossible to brace herself when she was at a disconcerting forty-five-degree angle. She gave up. Her only security was the pressure of his chest through the cardboard against her back.

"Shhh. Not so loud. Okay, here we go."

As the carton swayed with his movements, Liz tried to keep herself as still as possible. She willed the bottom not to drop out on her.

"What went wrong with your marriage?"

She jerked her head up at Matt's surprising question. At the same moment the box shifted and she loudly sucked in her breath.

"Liz, you don't have to tell me if it's too painful."

She realized he'd mistaken her gasp of fright as shock at his question. To her further surprise, she found herself wanting to tell him about Jonathan. "Actually it's only pride-bruising at this point. My ex-husband liked the idea of marrying his banker. Oh!"

The box was tilting more and more toward the left. Matt grunted and the box suddenly straightened again. She gave a sigh of relief.

"I'm sorry, honey," he said. "I was going around

the bush at the front of the garage. Now, about what's-his-face."

She smiled. "Jonathan. Let's just say he didn't like being a banker's husband when I wouldn't 'smooth over' certain banking irregularities for him."

"Irregularities?" The box tilted and righted again.

Liz swallowed. "Borrowing from inactive accounts to cover his own. Insuring loans for his company which would never qualify under normal circumstances. That sort of stuff. I was an assistant manager then, at a bank in Chicago, and Jonathan was climbing the corporate ladder any way he could. I always knew he was ambitious, but until we were married, I hadn't realized just how much."

"That bastard!"

She gave a dry chuckle. "I think I said that at the time. Among other things, especially after he was arrested."

The box suddenly dipped and was shifted upward in the same way an airplane reacts when it hits an air pocket. Liz swallowed again.

"He was arrested?" Matt asked.

"Just before the divorce was final. He'd found a willing partner at another bank. Since I was still married to him, the authorities wondered—"

"If you were involved," Matt finished for her. "Another set of bastards."

"I don't blame them," she said, but she smiled at his quick defense of her. "They were only doing their jobs."

"Well, they were idiots for thinking you were

part of it. At least now I understand why you're so paranoid about your reputation—"

"I'm not paranoid!" she snapped.

"And I figured there had to be a good reason why you were turned-off to men. . . ."

"I'm not 'off' men either!"

"Good. Then we can resume our 'discreet' meetings. I'll save some boxes for future visits."

With a bone-jarring thump she suddenly felt solid ground beneath the bottom of the carton. Then she was thrown from side to side as he turned the box around so the taped sides faced the hedge.

"Okay, sweetheart. All set. Give me a few seconds to get back into the house before you go through the hedge."

"Right," she muttered, trying to reorient herself after the spinning.

After counting to fifty she pushed hard against the side, and the tape gave. Crawling between the burst edges of the carton and scrambling through viciously scratchy twigs, she found herself blinking at the bright morning sunlight on her side of the hedge. Just to be sure, she reached out and touched the garden shed. Solid. Sighing in relief, she looked back at the hole Matt had cut in the middle of the hedge. It couldn't be any more than a foot wide, and she wondered how she'd managed to squeeze through it. All that mattered was that she had.

Hoping she had no audience for the rest of the farce, she rose to her feet and, since she didn't have a key to unlock the back door, casually walked around the house to the front. Along the way she tried to look as if she were admiring the roses, zinnias, and marigolds blooming with health. Nobody was outside, and, reaching the front porch, she picked up her morning paper and opened her door. After closing it behind her, she slumped against it for a long moment. Then she unslumped.

"The bank!"

Liz raced up the stairs even faster than she'd raced down them earlier. A glance at her bedroom clock told her she had ten minutes before the Brinks truck delivered cash to the bank. The time varied with each delivery, and this morning it was for eight o'clock. She was the only one who could sign for it, although that wasn't the only reason she'd turned down Matt's offer to stay at his house.

As she pulled the tie belt of her robe free, her hand brushed against the rose she'd stuffed into a pocket. She took it out and stared at it, then threw it into her bedroom wastebasket.

"Damn rose, and damn Matt," she cursed. "And what a hell of a morning."

Later that day Liz returned home from work and marched straight upstairs to the wastebasket. She stared at the rose lying inside, its petals looking limp and forlorn. Reluctantly she bent down and picked it up. She tossed it back into the can . . . and picked it out again.

"Damn rose," she muttered, laying it on her nightstand.

Six

Sitting in her swivel rocker, Liz gazed unseeing into the darkness of her living room. Silently she admitted what she didn't want to know.

She liked Matt Callahan.

Under the circumstances, she knew not liking him was the sensible course for her. After all, he'd put her in an almost untenable position several times. And throwing a woman out as the trash wasn't exactly the best way to make friends and influence people. Also, she wasn't thrilled with the way he'd given her the rose . . . or parked his car in her driveway for everyone to see . . . or . . .

She frowned. She could have sworn she had about forty different reasons not to like Matt, but at the moment she could think of only four, and she wasn't really angry about them anymore.

Now it was so easy to pinpoint Matt's good qualities. She had no doubt that he'd worked hard to gain the financial independence he'd achieved. He bought paintings because he liked them and not because the piece would enhance his ego or prestige. A square donkey with four noses touched his sense of whimsey. He had a sharp wit, with a mischievous-little-boy quality to his actions. Something deep inside her always stirred at the sight of his green eyes and roguish smile. He was concerned for her welfare. He'd given her a rose.

Settling farther into the plush velvet padding of the chair, Liz closed her eyes and smiled a tiny smile at the thought of the flower.

She wondered how many men would have had the audacity to break into a woman's house and leave a rose on her pillow. Probably not many. At least she was positive no sane man would. But Matt had a unique brand of sanity . . . or insanity. Whatever it was, he had made her emotions come alive as they never had before. She'd always had control over her temper—until she'd met Matt. Now she felt as though she were only taking a breather between rounds.

Her grin widening, Liz chuckled to herself. So far she'd already threatened death by auto, bare hands, and bull. If he only knew how often she meant to do him a bodily injury, he'd probably move to the opposite end of the state.

He was right, though, about her passionate nature. That was something she didn't know how to control. She'd never experienced it before, at least not to this degree. Her ex-husband had a good deal of outward self-assurance and sophistication, but he'd never inspired the highs and lows in her that Matt had. In fact, Matt was exactly the opposite of Jonathan. With deep certainty she knew

Matt never would have resorted to Jonathan's dirty methods to get ahead in the corporate world. She wasn't sure how she knew it; she just did. Matt might be a little devious at times, but there was a straightforward honesty about him. From the beginning he had told her he wouldn't allow her to ignore him, and since then he'd made sure she hadn't.

Matt's self-assurance came from inside, and not from his professional position. While the underwear ad indicated Matt had been a successful model, he certainly wasn't as well-known as Jim Palmer, the ball player. And yet he'd retired. From the way he was settling in next door, he was serious about it too. Jonathan's idea of gallantry had been to occasionally open a door for a woman. He certainly never would have dreamed up putting her in a box and carrying her out as trash to save her reputation.

Thinking about the morning's events, Liz giggled helplessly. In a box! The townspeople would have been shocked out of their woolies if they'd seen their very proper bank manager crawling through the hedge like a disheveled procupine. She burst into laughter as she imagined herself calmly brushing the twigs from her hair and saying, "Good morning, folks. Just examining the hedge for woodchucks. Have a nice day." She laughed even harder and wrapped her arms around her aching sides. Leave it to Matt to make a disaster into a laughing matter. The man really had a knack for it.

Liz's amusement faded when she imagined how well her bosses would have reacted to her explana⁺' ⌒n. She had the feeling that her best custo. ⌐r wouldn't be able to save her with them. Her luck had held one more time that morning, but she knew she'd stretched it far enough already.

She wondered briefly if Matt was right, and she *was* being paranoid about her reputation. If that were true, she had good reason after the fiasco with Jonathan. Although she had left the stain behind in Chicago, she had taken extra care with her image as an upstanding banker and employee. It would be months until a decision was made on who would replace Joe as district manager, and anything and everything she did would reflect on her ability to fill that position. The very last thing she wished to do was to make Joe or his judgment of her look poor, especially right before he retired. Joe deserved better. Now was definitely not the time to have met someone like Matt. Matt was dangerous and devilish and fun.

She hadn't been any of those things for a long time, Liz realized with an envying sadness. During college she'd set aside the little girl in her and become deadly serious about her goals in life . . . and dull. But Matt had brought out a facet of herself that had been hidden away long ago. As a bank manager she'd kept a polite distance between herself and the people of Hopewell. Not only had Matt ignored that distance, he'd insisted on closing it. Maybe that was why she continually lost her temper with him. He made her see Elizabeth O'Neal was something more than a one-dimensional bank manager. She was a woman with a highly charged emotional side and a little bit of mischief mixed into it. Unfortunately she hadn't been prepared to discover that about herself, but, at the moment, Matt had left her no option except to act upon it.

Glancing at the luminous dial of her wristwatch, she noted it was after midnight. She grinned again, this time in anticipation. Her "secret admirer" ought to be arriving soon with another surprise for her. And she was ready to catch him at it. Matt's denials hadn't fooled her in the least, and she felt deep in her bones that he was leaving the way open for his midnight courtship tactics. Well, she'd promised her "secret admirer" a little surprise in return, and she wouldn't disappoint him.

Liz stretched over the right arm of the rocker, her hand sinking into cool water. Satisfied the bucket of water she'd filled earlier was still cold enough for her purposes, she removed her hand and waved it in the air to dry it. Another chuckle escaped into the deep shadows of the room as she lit a cigarette and squinted against the bright flare of the match.

She hadn't managed to outwit Matt by fighting his games, but she might have a chance if she played along. So tonight, the image-conscious banker was gone and the little girl was returning once more.

Liz couldn't wait to see Matt's face when she did.

Dressed completely in black, Matt quietly stepped up to a side window of Liz's house and peered around an evergreen bush into the interior. He wasn't surprised by the sight of Liz's profile as she sat in the living room rocker. She was exactly where he expected her to be.

He grinned. If Liz was waiting for her "secret admirer," she was in for a disappointment.

He turned on his heel and headed around to the back of the house. Then he climbed up the porch steps and tapped lightly on the back door. The one person Liz probably didn't expect tonight, he thought, was her friendly next door neighbor, who was concerned only for her personal safety. . . .

When the back door opened, Matt instantly realized the one thing *he* hadn't expected was the wall of water shooting out of the bucket in Liz's hands. Before he could even think to duck, the water smacked him in the face and chest with a bone-shocking chill.

"Matt!" she exclaimed, her voice heavy with laughter. She set the bucket on the floor. "What a nice surprise."

He took a deep breath and very calmly wiped the water out of his eyes. "Good evening, Liz. I came over to borrow a towel."

"How apropos," she murmured between snorts that sounded suspiciously like giggles. "Come in, and I'll see if I have one."

Matt stepped into the dark kitchen, ignoring the loud squishing of his wet tennis shoes. He swiped a hand across his dripping beard, and droplets of water went flying in every direction.

"Your method of telling me I need a bath is a little extreme, don't you think?" he asked, eyeing her sourly.

She looked up from rummaging in a drawer on the other side of the room and shook her head.

"That bucket of water wasn't meant for you, Matt. It was intended for my 'secret admirer.' I wanted him to feel the full force of my admiration."

"I'll tell him it was a biggie."

"Do that," she replied, returning to him with a small dishtowel in her hand. "Here's your towel."

He glared at it, then took it from her and began drying his hair. "I don't suppose you could spare another."

Liz tapped her chin thoughtfully and surveyed him from head to toe. As he waited for her answer he could see the mirth filling her gray eyes, even in the darkened room. There were other differences that he sensed more than saw. The invisible defenses that usually bristled the air around her were gone, and she was relaxed and playful. It was as if she'd washed away her resistance when she dumped the water over his head. He decided it was worth a dousing just to see her this way.

"Matt, you look stunning," she finally said, and burst into laughter. "If only the advertising people could see you now."

"Advertising?" he questioned her in amazement.

"I saw the underwear ad you posed for," she explained, and began laughing again. "Right now you're perfect for the wet look."

He shook his head in disbelief, not noticing the clamminess of his jeans or the puddle forming at his feet. "You saw the underwear ad?"

"Mmmm. Why didn't you tell me before?"

"You were too busy yelling at me," he countered, then shrugged. "Besides, it's never come up in conversation."

"What about that day at the bank, when I asked you about your occupation."

"And I told you I'm retired. That's what I do now."

"Matt, that's as evasive now as it was then." Her amusement gone, she threw up her hands. "Forget it, my game-playing days are over. You've got your towel, now go home. It's late, and I want to go to bed."

There was something infinitely sexy about a woman telling a man she wanted to go to bed, Matt decided. Maybe it was the imagery the word *bed* conjured up in a man's mind that physically affected his body. But he had no need of his imagination to picture Liz lying on a bed. He'd seen the real thing.

Unfortunately his patience had rapidly dwindled with Liz's casual dismissal. It was time to let her know there was a payment for "the full force of her admiration."

Sternly he gazed at her for a long minute. Then he pulled the soaking wet turtleneck sweater over his head and dropped it onto the floor.

"Since you've so kindly washed my clothes," he said, "you can dry them too." Steadying himself with one hand on a kitchen chair, he gazed directly into her shocked, widening eyes as he began tugging off his tennis shoes. "You've got ten seconds to find me a towel bigger than a postage stamp, woman, or I'll strip *you* bare."

Liz didn't move until his second shoe hit the vinyl tiles, then she fled the room. Grinning, Matt pulled out the chair he was leaning against and sat down. It felt good to exert his rights as a man.

She probably would never let him get away with it again, but it felt good.

As Liz hurriedly gathered several large towels from the shelf of the upstairs linen closet, she cursed herself for her cowardice. Maybe if she had stayed and bluffed it out, Matt really wouldn't have . . . He would. Somehow he always managed to force her into acknowledging the physical attraction she felt for him.

She started laughing as she remembered what had caused the latest appearance of his machismo. The total astonishment on his face when she'd flung the bucketful of water at him had been more priceless than the Picasso he owned. She had to admit he had class for calmly asking to borrow a towel. Most people would have exploded in anger at her childish prank. And while it had been childish, she didn't regret it. It had felt good to have outwitted him for once. He'd probably never let her get away with it again, but it *had* felt good.

Returning to the kitchen, she was a little apprehensive as to his state of undress, and she peeked around the corner before entering. Seeing he was still in his jeans at least, she swept into the room and dumped her armful of towels onto his lap.

"Towels, as you requested, O mighty macho one," she said, her lips drawn back into a wide grin.

He draped one towel over his shoulders and stood. "The humility in your tone is quite touching. Have a good laugh upstairs?"

"After I was done cursing you," Liz chuckled again.

"Ahh," he murmured with a smile. "Now, that sounds promising."

"My cursing sounds promising?"

"Mmmm. Where's your dryer?"

She jerked her head up, startled. "My dryer?"

He nodded. "You know, the machine that whirls the clothes around until they're dry. You *are* drying my clothes."

"I am not!" she protested, her hands on her hips. "Go home and use your own."

"I really think you ought to reconsider," he suggested in silky tones. He picked up the bucket and walked over to the sink. "Otherwise, *you'll* be needing a towel."

"You wouldn't!"

He turned and gave her a look that said he most definitely would, then shoved the bucket under the tap. Liz blanched as he spun the cold faucet on full force. Water rattled loudly against plastic.

"Matt, the laundry room is to your left."

She sighed loudly with relief when he turned off the water. Cowardice had its place sometimes, she decided. Anyway, the wet look wasn't "in" this year.

"Smart girl," he said, patting her cheek as he passed her.

"Brilliant," she muttered, resisting the urge to shove her foot against his taut buttocks. Instead, she clenched and unclenched her hands in frustration.

The laundry room door closed behind him, and Liz soundly cursed herself. If only she hadn't insisted on playing his game! Now she was stuck with him while his clothes dried.

Groaning out loud, she couldn't believe he was actually in her house, stripping down to his bare skin.

"Oh, no!" she gasped, realizing Matt would be dressed only in a couple of towels when he re-emerged from that room. She had enough trouble controlling her physical and emotional reaction to him when he was clothed—but in a couple of towels!

Liz spun on her heel and ran for the stairs, intent on reaching her bedroom with its lovely stout lock on the door before Matt was aware she'd retreated in defeat. She acknowledged that not only did cowardice have its place on occasion, but it was also the only sensible means of survival sometimes.

And there'd better be a six-inch yellow streak running down her back right now, because she wouldn't give a wooden nickel for her chances of surviving Matt, she thought wildly. Her mother hadn't raised any stupid daughters.

In her dash through the living room Liz felt her panic ease as she caught sight of the staircase along the left wall. She ran toward it. Shifting mental gears, she slowed but still took the steps two at a time.

She was up the stairs in a flash and halfway down the hall before she heard a sudden noise behind her. Then a hand grabbed her arm and spun her around.

"Going somewhere?" Matt asked in a chiding voice.

Seven

He towered over her, dominating her senses with
his nearness. Dark curling hairs covered the wide
expanse of his upper chest. The towel draped
across his hard shoulders did nothing to hide his
physique. The muscles in his arms were lean and
hard rather than heavy. In the deep shadows of
the hallway his features were a mere outline of male
menace. But his green eyes were clearly visible, a
tender longing blazing in them.

Liz stared at him, all too aware of the towel that
barely covered his hips. She couldn't seem to
breathe, and her numbed brain couldn't find the
right command that would start her lungs working properly again. Her nostrils were filled with
the scent of subtle cologne and male flesh.

"I don't think I want to know where you were
going," he murmured when she didn't answer his
question. "But you were headed in the right direction for what I have in mind."

His words should have broken the spell holding her will in check, but they didn't. Instead, a hard shaft of desire shot through her, trapping her as effectively as his body did. She dimly realized the little girl in her had brewed more than one mischief tonight when she'd ignored the bank manager's common sense and propriety to play Matt's little-boy games. Now only the woman in her was left, helplessly responding to the man.

Matt slowly lowered his mouth to hers, his lips softly seeking her resistance. Cold reason clamored inside her for an instant, then vanished in an overwhelming rush of brightly colored sensations. Those sensations coursed through her veins, offering a sensual danger, a delicious fulfillment if she played out the game to its final goal. But those same heady sensations also promised peace and relief from all the restrictions imposed upon her. If only she dared to reach out. . . .

And why shouldn't she? Every woman deserved to follow her heart for one night, Liz thought in a haze of emotion. Every woman was entitled to one mistake. And in spite of feeling more like a female goddess of power, she was, after all, only a woman. An imperfect woman allowed her one mistake of a lifetime.

Well, if Matt was a mistake, at least he was a perfect one.

Pressing herself fully against him, she parted her lips, allowing him access for a more intimate game. As his tongue delved inside to mate with hers, she rushed to meet him in the give and take of the kiss. Her arms wrapped around his neck, her fingers burrowing under the draped towel to warm skin. She felt a deep pulling inside her that tightened her belly and thighs.

His lips seared hers, intent on drawing out all the passion of which she was capable. His body crowded her against the wall, his arousal cradling itself naturally in the junction of her legs. A strong hand cupped her breast, thumb rubbing insistently over her taut nipple.

Powerless at the churning emotions inside her, she clung to him. She didn't hear the low moan that issued from her own throat. The kiss was endlessly satisfying, yet still not enough. She wanted more. She wanted everything. With him.

Matt seemed to sense her thoughts at the same moment. For an instant his mouth dropped to the base of her throat, then he suddenly lifted her in his arms.

And turned around toward the stairs!

"But the bedroom's the other way," Liz blurted out, clutching his shoulders to steady herself.

His grin flashed whitely. "You have a wonderful sense of direction in the dark, Liz, but my clothes are downstairs in the dryer."

"But . . . I thought . . ."

"You thought what?"

She felt the heat radiating on her cheeks, then cleared her throat before stammering, "You . . . you know."

"Yes?"

"Stop playing dumb, Matthew Callahan! Now, put me down."

He just laughed and held her even more tightly as he descended the stairs. Furious and embarrassed, she swatted his bare shoulder.

"Behave, Liz, or I'll dump cold water on you to cool you off."

Narrowing her eyes at his amused features, she clamped her teeth together. Damn him! The man had ranted and raved for days about how they would make love. And now she had finally admitted he'd been right. She'd actually been in his arms, actually been ready to make love with him, and the last place he was interested in was the bedroom. She couldn't believe he could kiss her like that one moment and calmly walk away the next.

"You are a tease," she finally said.

He stopped on the bottom step and turned his head toward her. "I'm no tease, sweetheart. Unfortunately though, I realized that you are."

"Me?"

"Yes, you."

She pushed against his chest and he released her legs, letting her slip down his body. Even through her anger she could feel every inch of him burning into her own flesh. Her feet met the floor with an abrupt jolt, and she backed up a step.

"I was hardly teasing you. In fact, what happened between us was total honesty. Or do you constantly need the game-playing to get turned on?"

At her words the amusement vanished instantly from his face, and he glared at her. His body tensed and his hands curled into fists at his sides.

Liz sensed his temper was about to erupt, and she planted her feet firmly on the rug, ready to welcome it. Matthew Callahan could shout until he was hoarse. Then she'd tear into him for playing his stupid games and bruising her emotions beyond endurance.

Angrily he slashed the air between them with one hand. "You want honesty? I'll give you honesty. I stopped us from going to bed together because *you* weren't ready. It took everything I had to stop it, and believe me, honey, it was probably the hardest thing I've ever had to do in my life. I've watched you every day, watched you in your prim business suits going back and forth from the bank, knowing that there was a passionate woman underneath. Knowing that hidden woman was waiting there for me to let her out. But tomorrow morning you would have regretted what you'd done, and I knew it. That's why I stopped it. I want you, Liz, but I want you fully and completely and with no regrets."

She closed her eyes in self-recrimination. He was right. She hated to admit it, but he was right. She would have absolved herself afterward by blaming him. Still, knowing he'd done the right thing didn't stop the aching desire that continued to flood her body. Instead, she wanted him even more, simply because he cared enough to stop her from doing something she'd regret, no matter what the cost to himself.

"I think I hate honesty," she finally replied, opening her eyes.

Shaking his head, he chuckled dryly. "Not as much as I do."

He stepped off the bottom step and enfolded her in his arms. The embrace was comforting, and Liz laid her head on his chest.

"I'm still furious with you, you know," she said, slipping her arms around his bare waist.

"I'm not too thrilled with myself either," he replied, his fingers smoothing her hair.

And that was an understatement, he admitted silently. Knifelike physical pain had plunged through him when he'd pulled away from her. It had taken every ounce of his self-control to turn away from the bedroom. But he'd instinctively known, in spite of Liz's physical response, he'd only be seducing her. Somehow he hadn't been willing to follow in Don Juan's footsteps to that extent.

From the beginning Liz had been very special, and he wanted every part of her—mind, heart, body—with him all the way. Until that moment came, he was willing to wait.

He grinned, thinking of an old Billy Joel song. If only the good die young, then he'd be in his grave tomorrow for his saintly actions tonight.

And he had the feeling he'd be canonized before the week was out.

"So you're from Chicago," Matt called through the closed laundry room door.

Knowing he was in the process of dressing, Liz tried to suppress the butterflies in her stomach. In spite of the stout barrier between them, it was much too easy to remember his earlier attire. And how his body had heated hers.

"Not originally," she replied, backing up until she felt the counter edge digging into her back. "I was born and raised in Muncie, Indiana."

"I'm sorry. I didn't hear what you said."

"Muncie, Indiana," she repeated in a near screech, then groaned in disgust at the high-pitched nervousness in her voice.

"Farm country all the way. Why didn't you go back there after Chicago?"

With cautious steps she moved forward until she stood in the middle of the still darkened kitchen. "I don't know. I guess I didn't want my big brothers to cluck over me like a pack of mother hens."

"Ah."

She grinned wryly at his noncommittal remark. More than once she had cursed her fate of being the baby sister to three brothers. They had seen her as a little doll who would break at the slightest jarring, and she had never been able to convince them that she was as strong as they were. Their overprotectiveness would have been worse than ever if she'd gone back to Indiana after what had happened with Jonathan.

"Were you always from New York?" she asked, becoming curious about his background even though she knew she shouldn't. Knowing more about Matt could mean more reasons to like him, and she was afraid to like him more than she already did.

"Always," he answered. "Are you by any chance related to Tim O'Neal who plays left forward for the Pacers?"

Liz rolled her eyes heavenward at his astuteness. "Unfortunately that's big brother number three. Big brother number two was a fullback at

Notre Dame, and big brother number one played football for Annapolis."

The door suddenly swung open and Matt walked into the kitchen, stopping a few feet away from her. Fully clothed, he was still overpowering, and Liz's breath caught in her throat as she felt the full impact of him. It happened every time, she thought with a silent moan.

"You weren't kidding around when you said you had *big* brothers," Matt said.

"Very protective big brothers," she reminded him with a sweet smile. "I'd hate to think what they'd do to my 'secret admirer.' "

"Mmmm." Matt made a show of thoughtfully stroking his beard. "I suspect your 'secret admirer' won't be deterred by the prospect of three bruiser-type brothers. Fortunately though, you don't have to call on long distance protection. I'll be happy to provide all the protecting you want."

"I've never felt safer," Liz muttered.

"A jerky ex-husband and overprotective big brothers do explain quite a bit," he added.

She gasped. "What does that mean?"

"Your contradictions."

"My contra—!" she snapped, then stopped herself. He was deliberately throwing her off balance. Crossing her arms over her breasts, she asked, "And what about you? Where were you born? What about your family? Tell me how you got started in modeling. Maybe I can find some insights into *you*."

"I was born in the city," he answered promptly in an amused tone. "No family though. I started modeling when I was sixteen, and the work was hell, and the hours even more hellish, but the money was good. I graduated from NYU with a B.A. in economics. Night courses, of course. I like a good steak and a bottle of wine, chocolate ice cream, and spaghetti. Not necessarily served in that order. I like Pat Benatar, ZZ Top, Lionel Ritchie, and Phil Collins. I hate doing laundry. And you know how much money I have and that I invest in the commodities market on occasion. Anything else?"

She blinked, then shook her head. Dammit, she thought. He would have to like everything she liked.

"Good. By the way, which brother is the worst?"

She grinned at the casual sound of his voice. Evidently he'd begun to wonder about big brothers.

"Michael. Brother number two," she said, trying to control her rising laughter.

"The Notre Dame fullback? Pretty big, eh?"

"Actually it isn't Michael's size. It's his profession."

"What is he?" Matt asked, reaching up to caress her hair. "A bouncer? Cop? FBI? Kung fu expert?"

Joyfully anticipating the expected reaction, Liz let the words out slowly.

"Michael is a priest."

Matt's hand instantly dropped away. There was a very long pause as he digested the information.

"A priest."

"Wonderful guy," Liz said warmly, taking Matt's arm and guiding him to the back door. "Of course, he can be a bit intimidating at times. And he is conservative. Comes with the territory, I guess. I'll be sure and tell him how you're willing to come over at all hours of the night to protect me. Of the three, he's the one who worries the most about me."

Hiding her smile at Matt's stunned expression, she opened the back door and ushered him through it. "Good night, Matt."

"A priest!"

"Oh, yes. If all goes well, he'll soon be a monsignor—"

"Monsignor!"

"Say good night, Matt."

"Good night, Matt," Matt said, shaking his head in clear disbelief.

Liz shut the door in his face, then collapsed against the white-painted wood, her shoulders shaking with silent laughter.

Maybe she was better at the game than she'd thought.

Early morning sunlight filtered through the sheer white curtains as Liz rolled over to the other side of the bed.

It shouldn't be an empty one, she thought. Not after last night.

In a restless motion she flipped onto her back and opened her eyes. Staring sightlessly at the ceiling, she remembered exactly how Matt's mouth had fit so perfectly over hers. How fiercely his arms had tightened around her. How his hand had caressed her breast until she'd ached from wanting him . . . and how he'd lifted her in his arms and turned away from the bedroom.

"Damn you, Matt Callahan, for being so noble,"

"alluring"..."inspiring"...
"irresistible"...

Loveswept

EXAMINE 4 LOVESWEPT NOVELS FOR

15 Days FREE!

Turn page for details

America's most popular, most compelling romance novels...

Loveswept

Here, at last...love stories that really involve you! Fresh, finely crafted novels with story lines so believable you'll feel you're actually living them!

Read a Loveswept novel and you'll experience all the very real feelings of two people as they discover and build an involved relationship: laughing, crying, learning and loving. Characters you can relate to... exciting places to visit...unexpected plot twists...all in all, exciting romances that satisfy your mind and delight your heart.

And now you can be sure you'll never, ever miss a single Loveswept title by enrolling in our special reader's home delivery service. A service that will bring all four new Loveswept romances published every month into your home—and deliver them to you *before* they appear in the bookstores!

Examine 4 Loveswept Novels for

15 Days FREE!

To introduce you to this fabulous service, you'll get four brand-new Loveswept releases not yet in the bookstores. These four exciting new titles are yours to examine for 15 days without obligation to buy. Keep them if you wish for just $9.95 plus postage and handling and any applicable sales tax.

SEND NO MONEY NOW.
RETURN THIS
POSTAGE-PAID CARD TODAY!

FREE TRIAL/HOME DELIVERY ORDER CARD

Loveswept
Bantam Books, P.O. Box 985, Hicksville, NY 11802

☐ Please send me four new romances for a 15-day FREE examination.
If I keep them, I will pay just $9.95 plus postage and handling and any
applicable sales tax and you will enter my name on your preferred customer list to receive all four new Loveswept novels published each month
before they are released to the bookstores—always on the same 15-day
free examination basis.

20123

Name_____

Address_____

City_____

State_____Zip_____

My Guarantee: I am never required to buy any shipment unless I wish. I
may preview each shipment for 15 days. If I don't want it, I simply return the
shipment within 15 days and owe nothing for it.

F5678

she muttered, that same ache for him spreading through her again.

The only regret she felt now was that they hadn't made love. Shocking as the idea was, she acknowledged it with only a wry smile. She really ought to be feeling grateful this morning rather than perversely disappointed. She probably would have been feeling the opposite emotions if they had made love. After all, there was her image as a straight-laced banker, Joe's recommending her for the promotion, and her own qualms about having a relationship with a bank customer.

But, dammit all, it was her body and her decision whether or not to make love. And she had made a conscious decision to be with Matt. She'd known what was at stake, and she'd been willing to risk it all for him. Didn't he appreciate that? Didn't he understand that she *had* been ready? Didn't he realize the commitment she'd been ready to make to him? Even if she hadn't realized it until that moment, he should have known it.

She sat up in bed and pounded the mattress with an angry fist. "How dare he yell at me for not doing something and then yell at me for wanting to do it! I wonder how he'd like it if I did that to him!"

It would serve him right if she stuffed her "regrets" down his throat until he choked on them. If she sighed wistfully and said, "You were so right, Matt," every damn time she saw him. He'd regret ever opening his mouth about the subject. And it would drive him crazy if she acted about as regretful as a cat who'd found a stash of catnip.

An evil chuckle escaping her, Liz threw back

the covers and slid out of bed. She quickly padded over to her closet, opened the louvered doors, and surveyed her wardrobe with critical eyes.

She shook her head at the black cocktail dress with the plunging neckline. Too obvious, and besides, she couldn't wear it to the bank. The forest-green wool with the long sleeves had possibilities, but it might be too warm later in the day.

"There has to be something," she muttered, flipping through the hangers.

Subtlety was what she needed. Something subtle, and yet seductive . . .

"Ah-ha!"

She pulled out a vivid pink silk blouse and held it up to the room's growing light. Perfect! Then she picked out a mauve suit, knowing its pencil-straight skirt was cut deliberately tight across the hips.

Hanging them over the top of the closet door, she headed for the bathroom.

Fifty minutes later she slipped on her highest heels and straightened, glancing over to the full-length mirror to check on her results.

"Oh, my," she gasped in surprise.

There was definitely a subtle allure to the way her blond hair just brushed her shoulders. By lining both her upper and lower eyelids, she had made her eyes seem larger. In contrast, her other features seemed even more delicate and fragile-looking. She'd turned up the collar of her shirt and left the first three buttons undone. The effect was sophisticated yet sexy. With no bra, the small, full slopes of her breasts were noticeable, and her nipples stood out darkly under the semi-transparent silk shirt. The skirt seemed glued to her hips and thighs.

"Once you get to the bank, *don't* take off the jacket!" she warned her reflection.

She picked up the oversize suit jacket and left the bedroom. Her strides were shorter than usual because of the tight skirt, and her step slower because of the height of her heels. Her walk wasn't awkward, but she prayed she wouldn't break an ankle as she carefully made her way down the stairs.

In the kitchen she dropped her jacket over a chair and picked up the sugar bowl. Opening the lid, she frowned at the glittering crystals that nearly reached the brim.

"Can't have that."

She walked over to the counter and dumped the sugar back into the proper canister, which was three-quarters full already. Then, taking a deep breath and clasping the empty bowl in front of her, she marched through the house and out the front door.

Matt didn't know it, but he was about to sweeten her morning, she thought, then grinned. He'd sweeten it in more ways than one.

Eight

"I'm coming!" Matt shouted as he hurried down the stairs.

Slipping his arms into the sleeves of his blue cambric shirt, he wondered why someone always telephoned or came to the door while a person was in the bathroom. There must be something in bathroom doors that sent out a radar signal— bathroom occupied, send attack force now.

Grinning to himself, he began to button his shirt with one hand and opened the door with the other.

"I'll be damned," he breathed, his hand freezing on the top button.

"Good morning, Matt," Liz said.

The words were a simple greeting, but the delivery sounded as though she were on the other side of a bed than on the other side of the threshold. Her blouse was a wisp of nothing, and the junction of her legs was outlined in a deep V by her tight skirt.

His heart thumping erratically, he was positive he'd never seen a banker look so sexy. Liz gave new meaning to the words "rising interest."

"I was wondering if I could borrow some of yours," she said.

He dragged his eyes away from her too visible breasts.

"What?"

"I need a little sugar, Matt."

For a moment he thought she was asking for a kiss, until he finally noticed the bowl she was holding in one hand.

"Sugar. Of course."

He didn't move away from the door, his attention recaptured by her breasts. Both nipples were raised by the cool morning air. He had a strong urge to rip the blouse from her and taste the sweet flesh underneath.

"Matt? The sugar?" she prompted him. The sugar bowl she was offering suddenly hid the splendid view he'd been admiring.

Blinking, he realized she'd wanted only to borrow some sugar. Motioning her inside, he took the bowl from her hand. As she walked by him he found himself intently watching the provocative swing of her hips.

"Matt?"

"Mmmm?"

"Shut the door."

Abruptly Matt came to his senses and gave a silent curse at his gawking reaction to her. He shut the front door and reluctantly raised his gaze to her face. A knowing smile played on her lips, and her eyes held a look of pure feminine triumph.

He squinted at her in disbelief. Liz dressed like an ad for Frederick's of Wall Street? Borrowing sugar from him? And in broad daylight?

What the hell was going on around here?

Feeling a hasty retreat was his wisest course of action, Matt headed for the kitchen. Once there, he dumped a scoopful of sugar into the bowl, crystals spilling down the sides and onto the blue tile counter. He didn't bother to clean up the mess as dozens of reasons for Liz's sudden morning visit collided in his brain. But one thought was uppermost. If she was out of sugar, then he was a Martian. Struggling for some thread of logic to explain her enticing appearance and sultry behavior, he discovered he couldn't find one. Not one innocently logical explanation for her presence occurred to him. There wasn't any, he concluded.

Her abrupt change in attitude meant only one thing. Liz was up to something.

Sugar forgotten, Matt turned around and leaned back against the counter. Crossing his arms over his chest, he stared at the octagonal wall clock, all the while wondering what the hell she could be up to. He dismissed the idea that she could be trying to provoke a sexual response from him. She already knew he was interested. In fact, he was more than interested with her dressed like that. It was a monumental effort *not* to carry her off to the bedroom.

Was she teasing him after last night? She should

know he wouldn't give a damn about three big brothers, whatever their professions. Father Michael had been only a momentary shock. Was she attempting reverse psychology on him to scare him off? If so, it was causing the opposite effect.

Rubbing a hand across his forehead, he groaned in frustration. Liz wasn't a devious person. She had always been honest with him. Sometimes too honest, but she never played games to entice a male . . . at least she didn't with him. Wearing a sheer blouse with no bra didn't mean anything. There were a lot of women who didn't even own a bra.

His thoughts were interrupted when Liz entered the kitchen and walked toward him. "How do you like Hopewell so far?" she asked.

"Fine, fine," he replied, straightening up from the counter. He stared at her breasts, hoping she wouldn't cross her arms over them, and at the same time praying she would.

"Good. Very good."

He knew he had to have imagined the wanton purr in her voice. It wasn't really there. She stopped close beside him and began brushing the spilled sugar together into a small pile. Although her breasts were no longer in his line of vision to torture him, her light perfume filled his nostrils, and her arm and hip brushed lightly but rhythmically against him with her movements.

"I want to thank you for being such a gentleman last night," she said, finally breaking the silence

Her voice was low and breathy, and Matt tried

to ignore the alluring sound of it. He gave her a sharp nod in reply.

"I really appreciate the sugar. Small towns are so warm and friendly, aren't they? Not like big cities."

"It's why I moved here," he answered, feeling the topic of conversation was about as unsexy as it could get. Liz certainly wasn't. "I always wanted to live in a small town."

Her gray eyes were wide as she turned toward him and murmured, "I'm so glad you picked Hopewell."

He stared at her in shock. She's been fighting him since the first moment they'd met, and now she was acting as if she couldn't wait to hop into bed with him. Suddenly he was furious with her for confusing the hell out of him.

"What is wrong with you?" he shouted, pointing an accusing finger at her. "You're dressed like a hooker and cooing like a stuffed pigeon this morning. Did you take an idiot pill or something?"

She looked at him for a long minute, then calmly said, "I have no idea what you're so angry about, Matt. I'm only dressed as usual for work—"

"You have never worn *that* to work!"

"Yes I have, although I haven't worn it since you've moved here. It's nice and cool—"

"That's an understatement."

"And it still looks good at the end of the day, so it can double for evening wear," she continued, ignoring his caustic comment. "I'm not 'cooing,' either. I'm simply being pleasant this morning. Evidently *you* are not pleasant in the morning—"

"What the hell does 'evening wear' mean?" he asked suspiciously.

She gave an indulgent chuckle. "I thought you used to be in the fashion business. It means I can wear it to a restaurant for dinner, or to a show. . . ."

"Do you have a date?" he began, an urge to murder rising in him. "Because if you do, you can just break it—"

"*Moi?* Have a date?" She picked up the sugar bowl. "Thank you for the sugar, Matt. I'll see myself out."

Straightening, he grabbed her arm before she could move. "Do you have a date, Liz? Just answer me that."

She smiled a tiny half smile. "Only with my 'secret admirer.' I've discovered he's a man *to* admire."

Bewildered by her answer, he let her go as she pulled away from him and strolled leisurely out of the kitchen.

Questions slammed around in his brain as Matt watched her disappear through his dining room. Was she inviting him back for another midnight rendezvous? Was she ready to make love? Or would he get another face full of water?

What the hell was going on around here?

Lying on her bed, her head propped against the headboard, Liz watched the eleven o'clock news anchorwoman sign off for the evening. Over an hour ago she'd pulled the portable TV to the foot of her bed, and its phosphorescent glare was the only illumination in her darkened bedroom.

As a commercial began, Liz straightened for a moment and rubbed at the ache that had settled in her neck. Then she tucked the long silk nightgown of midnight blue around her ankles. Even though she felt tired, she knew she wouldn't be able to sleep. The morning events with Matt kept playing through her head.

She lay back against the upright pillows and scowled, wondering what had possessed her to stroll over to his house and ask to "borrow" a cup of sugar. She must have been out of her mind! It certainly wasn't difficult to understand why Matt had thought she was dressed like a hooker. The pink blouse was nearly as transparent as plastic wrap.

A tiny grin curving her lips, she silently admitted Matt hadn't been indifferent to her outfit. The look on his face when he'd opened his door had been priceless.

Thank heavens, though, her not-so-secret admirer hadn't accepted her invitation to come over this evening, she thought as her grin faded. At least one of them had some sense amid all the nonsense they'd been playing on each other lately. She only wished it had been *her* common sense that had surfaced just before she'd walked out of her house with that damn sugar bowl.

She shook her head, knowing she shouldn't be less grateful to Matt simply because she'd made a fool of herself. After all, she was a grown woman, and she shouldn't have acted like a perverse child who immediately did something she'd been told not to.

An odd kind of disappointment surfaced within

her, and Liz grimaced as she tried to suppress it. But the disappointment grew stronger. She finally admitted that she would happily have tossed all responsibility for her actions out the window if Matt had shown up that evening. Of course, he'd seen to it that she wouldn't have to make that choice now.

She sighed as she watched the late night show logo stream across the small TV screen. When she saw that the movie was *Captain Blood,* her spirits rose. She'd always been a fan of the old movies, especially pirate movies, and especially Errol Flynn pirate movies. Although she'd seen it seven or eight times before, she decided to watch it again. She had nothing better to do, and maybe a good rousing adventure would finally make her sleepy.

"Did I miss anything?" Matt asked, strolling into her bedroom as if it were the public library.

At the sound of his voice Liz screamed and leaped off the bed, terror pounding through her veins. In the same second she recognized Matt, and she placed a trembling hand to her chest to calm her wildly beating heart while her breath bellowed in and out of her lungs.

"What are you doing here?" she demanded in a gasping voice as she slumped in relief.

"I came over to watch the movie with you," he explained, stopping at the other side of the bed. He was dressed completely in black again, as he'd been the night before.

"Well, you scared me half to death. I didn't even hear you in the hallway."

He chuckled. "I guess I should have announced

myself, but I wanted to surprise your 'secret admirer.' " He looked around the room. "Where is he?"

"Wherever he is, he's definitely not all there," she muttered. She walked over to the closet, pulled out a blue flowered cotton robe, and shrugged into it. Quickly buttoning the robe's front, she asked, "What *are* you doing here?"

"I came to watch the movie." He held up a large brown paper bag she hadn't noticed in her terror. "I brought popcorn and beer."

She couldn't stop the sudden giggle that escaped her. Leave it to Matt to cart over refreshments while he put on a fright show for her.

"You'll ruin everything by being here when my 'secret admirer' shows up," she pointed out.

"That's the general idea. Mind?" he asked, dropping the bag on top of the bed. Without waiting for her answer he sat on the edge of the mattress, yanked off his jogging shoes, then slid toward the bed's center and crossed his legs Indian-style. "You know, Liz, you really ought to have all the locks on your doors changed. It's too damn easy to get into your house."

"I never had any problems with intruders before," she replied sourly. "Until you moved next door. I wonder why that is."

"You didn't have me before to point out these little things to you." He opened the bag, pulled out a smaller plastic one, then held it toward her. "Popcorn?"

Her shock completely gone, she knew this was the moment to ask him to leave. She would be breaking all her own personal rules if Matt stayed in her bedroom a moment longer.

"With butter?" she asked, curious.

He arched his brows. "Popcorn without butter is like the Empire State Building without King Kong."

She felt her resistance ebb at the thought of hot buttered popcorn to go with the movie. Gingerly sitting down on the very edge of the bed, she reached inside the plastic bag and scooped up some popcorn. "Thanks."

Munching on the salted and buttered ambrosia, she wryly decided that Matt thrived on the outrageous. It must be contagious, because the situation couldn't get any more bizarre than the adult pajama party she was now hosting. Unfortunately she was the only one who'd dressed properly. She swallowed heavily.

"Like a beer?" Matt asked, breaking into her thoughts.

She turned to look at him and found he was watching the movie intently. He was more interested in Errol Flynn's exploits than he was in her, she told herself. Embarrassment heated her face. The tension in her body dissipated, though, with the knowledge that he wouldn't suddenly begin to pillage and plunder her.

"A beer would be fine," she replied, briefly wondering at the vague regret she felt inside her. She sternly told herself she didn't *want* to be pillaged and plundered by Matt—and immediately suppressed the voice inside her that called her a liar.

Without taking his gaze from the screen he popped the tab on a frosted beer can and handed it to her. Scooting more fully onto the quilted spread, she carefully crossed her legs while keeping her nightgown and robe in place with her free hand. After giving him an unnoticed grin, she lifted the can to her lips and sipped the smooth, tangy beer.

"How long have you been breaking into women's houses to watch the late movie?" she asked, balancing the can between her crossed ankles.

"Since I retired from modeling and moved next door. Hey! Gimme back the popcorn."

"In a minute," she replied, pouring enough popcorn for six people onto her lap. She handed back the bag. "Don't worry. I left you some."

"Not much," he grumbled, shaking the bag to check its now depleted contents. Then he peered at her and asked, "How long have you been sharing popcorn and beer with men?"

She choked on some popcorn, then sipped more beer to help clear her throat. Leaning to her right and placing the beer can on the floor this time, she turned her head and answered, "Since you retired and moved next door. Matt, why are you doing this?"

"For the same reason you are," he replied, his eyes turning greener as they stared into hers.

She glanced away hastily. "My excuse is that you're insane and I'm just humoring you until the men with the butterfly net arrive."

"Let's hope they don't come until the movie's over. Now, be quiet! This is the best part. Flynn's about to escape from the island prison and start swashing his buckle all over the place."

Bursting into laughter, Liz fell back onto the

mattress. Popcorn shot into the air, showering her and Matt in a short blizzard of fluffy kernels.

"I wish someone had told me it snows in Vermont in July," Matt said, calmly brushing popcorn off his black shirt and jeans.

Her laughter subsiding into giggles, Liz raised herself on her elbows. "Only in the higher elevations, like second floor bedrooms. Did I miss any buckles swashing?"

"Not yet," he said as he turned his head and grinned at her. He began to brush popcorn off her, his right hand briskly skimming her body at first, then slowing to long, smooth strokes.

Liz felt her unvoiced protest die at his movements. She couldn't move, couldn't tear her gaze from his handsome bearded face. His hand gently explored her slender legs through her gown. It evoked a shivering response that left her wanting more. Then his hand rose higher, burning a path up her hipbones and waist before it settled on her breast and kneaded the soft flesh. The distinctively colored sensations she'd felt once before were back again, but stronger this time, entrapping her in their brightness. Of their own accord her head dropped back and her eyes closed. In a daze she felt the bed shift as Matt twisted around until his body was hard against hers.

His mouth suddenly covered her own, his arms wrapping around her in a tight embrace. Lips fused, tongues moved rhythmically. The kiss was white-hot with mutual want and need.

Caught up in its intensity, Liz moaned in the back of her throat as her hands automatically slid around his shoulders. Her nails sank into the black shirt. She could feel the heat of Matt's skin, and her own flesh burned in response.

She gave a helpless cry of protest when he lifted his head for an instant. Then he pressed his face into the base of her slender neck, his lips caressing the sensitive flesh.

"I thought you came over to watch Errol Flynn," she whispered, feeling a reluctant duty to remind him of the reason for his visit.

"Flynn can wait," he murmured against her skin. "You and I can't."

"I know," she replied, the last of her resistance crumbling.

At her acknowledgment Matt felt his blood surge through him. He reached up and began to unbutton her robe, all the while silently cursing his awkward movements. Liz's hands suddenly touched his, soothing them. His fingers finally unbuttoned the robe and, sitting up, he deftly slipped her out of it. The nightgown swiftly followed.

"We're covered in popcorn," he muttered inanely, gazing at the tiny splendor of woman that she was. "Lord, but you're beautiful."

She chuckled, then her large gray eyes drifted closed as he began to trace patterns across her chest and shoulders. Her wheat-colored hair was fanned out against the pillow, and his fingers couldn't resist wandering through the silky strands.

"Your clothes," she murmured, and slid her palms from his shoulders to his shirtfront.

He removed her hands, and she sucked in her breath at the speed with which he shed his clothes and tossed them over the side of the bed. He turned back to her, his eyes greener than summer leaves. Even if she'd wanted to, she couldn't have taken her gaze off him. His face exuded passion, his eyes hypnotizing with tenderness. A dense swath of curling dark hairs spread across his chest and arrowed down his belly and below. His thighs were rock hard.

He was total male, dominating her feminine senses. His primitive masculinity called to something deep inside her that had never been touched before but had long waited for this moment.

Mindlessly she rose up and pressed her body into his. Wrapping her arms around his back, she rested her cheek against his hot skin and whispered, "Matt, please love me now."

With a harsh groan he crushed her down into the bed. He kissed her, his tongue instantly finding and mating with her own. His hands were strong and sure as they stroked her breasts, his fingers coaxing her nipples to exquisite points.

Liz felt as if she were being turned inside out from the maddening torture. Nothing could be more satisfying and yet unsatisfying than what was happening to her body. His mouth suddenly dropped to her breasts, covering first one then the other with frenzied kisses. He took each aroused nipple between his lips, slowly swirling his tongue around the tight buds. His hand skimmed lower to her restlessly shifting legs, then his fingers caressed her with a gentle roughness that left her gasping.

His name tumbling from her lips in unconscious litany, she clung to him as her rock against the turbulence building inside her. She wanted to return his caresses, make him feel the overwhelming hunger she was feeling. But she could only hold tight and respond to him.

With no warning his mouth was on hers again, his hips suddenly forcing their way between her thighs. In the next instant he thrust himself inside her, and she shuddered at the feel of their oneness. Wrapping her legs around his waist, she easily adjusted to his length.

"Liz, Liz," he murmured, his lips almost biting kisses into her throat. "I've never felt something was so right as now."

"Nothing ever was," she said in a breathless whisper.

And it *was* right, she thought as they began to move together. Her hips matched each movement of his with a perfection so rare that she wondered helplessly at it. He had always seemed to know exactly where to touch her and how. But now . . . now the touch was more than physical. It left no part of her hidden, and she felt the emotional bonds tighten around her heart as surely as she felt the commitment in her body that only a woman can give to a man.

As if sensing her final surrender to him, Matt curved his hands around her buttocks and pulled her impossibly close against him. He drove into her repeatedly, taking her higher than she'd ever gone before. Bright lights exploded in her mind, and she convulsed in his arms as an unparalleled pleasure flooded her veins.

Thrusting once more, Matt called out her name. He held her tightly for endless minutes, his own pleasure prolonged and intense.

Finally Liz drifted back down to earth and

became aware of his body lying heavily on hers. His head was nestled into her shoulder, his arms still tight around her. Their damp skin seemed almost welded together, and she smiled at the thought. Nothing would separate them now. She wouldn't fight him any longer; there'd been nothing to fight except her own silliness. All along Matt had voiced the truth of her feelings.

Well, almost all of them. She was in love with him. Everything fell into place now that she'd finally acknowledged it. It explained all the ups and downs she'd been going through, all the perverse craziness he so easily evoked in her. And, of course, he loved her. That was the only logical explanation for his constant pursuit of her.

Savoring the knowledge, she lovingly stroked the steely muscles of his back. She'd tell him how much she loved him in a moment, she decided, and then he'd tell her he felt the same. Naturally they would have to work out how their relationship would progress from this point on, but she wasn't worried. Matt had an imagination that would put Walter Mitty to shame.

But right now she wanted only to hold him, caress him, and take pleasure in knowing she loved and was loved in return.

"I'm probably smashing popcorn into your back," he muttered as he released her and rolled onto his side.

She managed a watery chuckle, her emotions cresting inside her. She turned toward him and curled an arm around his neck.

"I don't care." She kissed his chest. "I never felt anything like that before, Matt."

He reached up with a finger and raised her chin. Bending his head, he gave her a tender kiss. "Neither have I, sweetheart. It was perfect."

She sighed. How she loved him!

But before she could open her mouth, he swiveled around and leaned over the edge of her bed. Sitting up, he began pulling on his briefs.

Incredulous, she sat up and stared at him as he slipped on his jeans. Finally she found her voice. "What are you doing?"

"I'm getting dressed," Matt replied, shrugging into his shirt.

Nine

"You're . . . you're getting dressed?" Liz repeated in astonishment as Matt quickly buttoned his shirt.

"Socks and everything," he said cheerfully over his shoulder while holding up one of his black socks and waving it at her. Then he bent to put on the sock.

At the sight of his back turned toward her, Liz felt a wild fury burst inside. Without thought she curled her hand into a fist and whacked him between the shoulder blades.

"Hey!" he yelped, leaping off the bed. He whipped around to face her. "What the hell was that for?"

"That was for getting dressed!" she shouted, scrambling off the mattress. "How dare you make love to me and get dressed afterward!"

He gazed at her for a moment before patiently saying, "I don't think you'd be very happy if I walked buck naked out of your house. Of course, I could be wrong about all this—"

"Why are you going at all?" she demanded, placing her fists on her hips. She silently vowed to kill him after she got the answer. She wanted only to hear it first, just to see how outlandish it would be.

"I'm going for you," he told her, crossing his arms over his bare chest. "If I don't go now, I know I'll never get out of that bed again. And I'll never let you out of it either. Think about it, Liz, and think about what you really want."

Her anger drained at his unexpected words, and she unconsciously slumped as her arms dropped to her sides. She wasn't sure what she wanted. Her job at the bank was important to her, and she didn't want to risk losing it. She didn't want to let Joe down after he'd recommended her to replace him. She had the good will of the townspeople, and she didn't want to lose that either.

But she wanted Matt to stay.

Confused and feeling defeated, she sat on the edge of the bed. Almost absently she picked up her robe and slipped it on. Staring down at her toes she muttered, "I wish you'd stop leaving all these major decisions up to me."

"It's a dirty job, but somebody's got to do it," he said. Sitting next to her, he curved an arm around her shoulders. "Besides, if I acted like 'macho man,' you'd have all the fun of blaming me for tonight and tomorrow morning. Now I can blame you for being a contrary female."

"Stinker," she murmured affectionately, leaning against his chest.

She couldn't love him any more than she did at that moment, Liz thought. Obviously it hadn't been easy for him to leave her bed, but he had done it out of concern for her reputation. He was willing to sacrifice his male pride to her, to let her decide each step of their relationship. She had outside responsibilities and obligations, and he was bowing to them. A woman never had a more caring lover and friend than she had in Matt.

But she wouldn't tell him she loved him just yet, she decided, smiling a tiny smile. He'd have to say the words first—all liberated males were secure enough to say "I love you" before a woman did.

And she was entitled to a little revenge for his being such a damned liberated and noble male.

As Liz snuggled closer and wound her arms around his waist, Matt closed his mind against the sudden urge to take her again. It really had been too soon for them to make love, and yet he sensed how much Liz had opened up to him emotionally. But he knew he'd ruin everything at this point if he rushed her.

He'd never been more serious about anything when he'd said he'd never let her out of the bed. She was heaven wrapped up in a tiny package of passionate dynamite and feminine softness. And he loved finding that dynamite and softness behind the prim, all-business exterior she normally projected. He loved her lightning temper. He loved her gray eyes, and the way they mirrored her moods.

Matt cursed silently. He never should have come over, but he hadn't been able to resist her cryptic invitation. And he'd been an idiot to think he could keep the night innocent by bringing popcorn and beer. Still, nothing had seemed more innocent than popcorn, beer, and a late night pirate movie. Nothing had been less innocent than the sight of Liz dressed in a clinging nightgown. At first he'd managed to keep himself in check, but then she had spilled the popcorn. . . .

Instantly he tried to suppress the memories of their lovemaking, but they swirled in his brain in sensual Technicolor. Last night he'd foolishly thought he'd been ready for sainthood for *not* making love to her. But now he knew better. He groaned silently. Oh, brother, did he know better! Liz was right; being noble stunk.

"I have to go," he finally said, forcing his arms to drop away from her.

She didn't move. "Wait until the movie's over."

He involuntarily glanced over at the TV screen and groaned aloud. Captain Blood was kissing his woman into submission. The last thing he needed to see was a macho man doing things his way. To Matt's relief, a commercial broke in on the sizzling moment. He wished someone had cut in with a commercial when Liz had spilled the popcorn all over them. Then he would have been saved this agony.

It was sheer torture to feel her body pressed against his and to know only thin cotton kept his hands from her silkiness. And worse, he remembered all too well how she had melded perfectly to his own burning flesh during their lovemaking.

"I *have* to go," he stated, jumping to his feet.

Liz tumbled to the floor. Immediately contrite, he helped her to stand. "I'm sorry, sweetheart."

"When you gotta go, you gotta go," she replied as she pushed her hair back from her face.

There was a sudden awkward silence, and he wasn't sure how to fill it. Should he ask about the next step in their relationship? Or should he just wait for her to say something? Machismo occasionally had its good points, he decided.

When Liz still wouldn't meet his eyes, he realized she had no idea what to say either. He pulled her to him and repeated, "I'm going for you. You do know that, don't you?"

She chuckled against his chest. "I could always carry you out with the trash tomorrow morning."

Head and shoulders above her and seventy pounds heavier, Matt burst into laughter at the thought of her trying to carry him out in a box. When his laughter finally subsided, he patted her back and said, "Leave the hernias to me."

As she disentangled herself from his embrace, he heard her mutter, "You're no fun." Louder, she said, "Thanks for protecting me from my 'secret admirer,' Matt. I don't know what I would have done without you."

A dry chuckle escaped him as he shook his head. "You probably would have spilled popcorn all over the poor guy and then made mad passionate love with him."

He couldn't help grinning when he saw a scarlet blush spread across her cheeks and down her throat. Her eyes narrowed, and he instantly wiped all humor from his face. No sense having a bottle of beer dumped on him this time, he thought in wry amusement.

She gave him a saccharine smile. "You can tell him what he missed."

As she turned and led the way out of the bedroom, Matt gave a last resigned look at the disheveled bed before picking up his shoes and following her.

"He already knows," he muttered to her back.

Liz needed a cigarette.

Joe flipped over the last computer printout of the bank's monthly receipts, and pushed the folder to the side of her desk. "I see you're completely on line now with the mainframe computer at the central office. I'm sorry it took so long."

She shrugged. "I didn't expect my branch to be computer-connected to Central for a while yet. After all, we're pretty small and out of the way."

"This is my fastest-growing branch, and you should have had first priority," Joe replied forcefully. "And you have the responsibility of handling the accounts for the Milk Maid Processing plant. Sometimes I think Central sits on its collective brains." He leaned forward in his chair. "Liz, there are some things being said by a few peabrains that I think you ought to know."

She tensed, her mind reeling with dreaded speculation. Her most acceptable thought was that Joe was going to fire her. Her worst was that somebody twenty feet tall had peeked through her bedroom window the night before and was now calling everyone in the western hemisphere to announce what he'd seen. If ever there was a time for a cigarette . . .

"Yes?" she finally croaked out, and immediately cleared her throat. It didn't help, and she felt the parched scratchiness all the way down to her stomach.

"When I suggested you to replace me after I retire, the bank directors were pretty enthusiastic about it." Joe made a face. "But yesterday Ford Carson made a comment about your age hampering you with the other managers, in spite of your accomplishments with this bank."

"Oh . . . ah . . . well, don't worry about it, Joe," she stammered, feeling a great weight beginning to lift off her. It wouldn't be Joe's fault or hers if the directors decided not to give her the job because of her age. That was just discrimination, and, under the circumstances, she had no urge to fight it. "With my low seniority at the bank, I really am a dark horse candidate—"

"That has nothing to do with it!" he interrupted, waving a dismissing hand at her words. "You are the *best* person for the job, and those idiots know it."

"Joe, Joe," she said with a desperate laugh. "As Mr. Carson pointed out, I'm young and, frankly, I've been a little worried about whether I'm too inexperienced for the job. In another couple of years, maybe then . . ."

In spite of Joe's angry gaze she managed a smile. She kept smiling when he didn't answer her at first.

"You've never realized just how good you are at your job, have you, Liz?" he finally asked, and without waiting for an answer continued. "This branch is the most efficient and the most profitable of the six that I oversee. And, I believe the credit can go to you.

She shrugged again, not knowing what to say. She'd never felt so confused. Somehow her priorities were changing, and while she wasn't sure what order they'd finally take, she did know they would never be the same again.

Matt had done this to her. He'd broken into her quiet, dull life just as easily as he'd strolled into her bedroom with his damn popcorn and beer. He stirred her body, stirred her emotions, made her fall in love with him despite all her resistance. She would have liked to claim that her response to him was only physical, a simple, long-denied need to be a woman in the most fundamental way. But it wasn't. The game had been played out, and she had fallen in love.

Out of all the confusion, though, one thought was uppermost in her brain. Last night Matt had never once said he loved her. He'd said everything but that. She tried to dismiss his omission— after all, there'd been no time, there had been other things to discuss—but she found she couldn't. "I love you" was such a short phrase. Three small words . . .

"Liz, don't let it worry you."

"But it takes only a second to say them," she mumbled, then realized it was Joe who had spoken, and not some little voice in her head. Coughing to hide her embarrassment, she hastily added, "Just a tickle in my throat. I really appreciate what you've done for me, but it's up to the board now, and you know how they can be."

Joe put up a hand, stopping her words. "I'm sorry I told you, but I did want you to be aware of what one of the directors might be thinking about your replacing me."

"And I thought I had left corporate back-biting behind me in Chicago," she commented with a chuckle.

Joe laughed. "I came here from D.C. thirty years ago for the country air and relaxing lifestyle. Sometimes I think I would have gotten a few less ulcers back in D.C."

Liz grinned at him.

"Well, enough of brainless idiots." Joe lifted his briefcase onto the desk and opened it. He handed her a sealed envelope. "Here's the new Brinks schedule for the month."

"This is different," she said, looking at the envelope. Usually she'd just receive a phone call the day before from Joe to give her the time of a cash delivery.

He snapped the locks of the case shut before saying, "There've been a few misunderstandings about delivery times, so Central decided to set up a schedule."

She saw a look of disgust cross Joe's face, and couldn't help agreeing with him. Setting up cash deliveries on a monthly basis, and worse, having it committed to paper meant more people would be aware of the delivery times.

"What am I supposed to do with the schedule?" she asked curiously. "Commit it to memory and burn it afterward?"

"Some clown actually suggested that," Joe replied sarcastically. "You just have to initial it as being received and read, and then lock it in the bank's own safety deposit box. At the end of the month you have to mail it back to Central."

"This isn't going to work, Joe," she said as she reached for a pen. "Not that the calls were much better."

"Short of wearing raincoats and meeting in dark alleys, nothing's really better. But I like this method less than the calls. Too many people will see *all* the branch schedules, and I'm afraid someone might get greedy. Very greedy."

It was her turn to make a face. "And you want to give me your job *now*? Thanks a lot, Joe. You're a real friend."

He chuckled and stood up. "I better get out of here before you have me thinking I'm pulling a dirty trick on you. Anyway, you've got a customer."

Rising, Liz glanced over her shoulder at the lobby area. Seeing the woman who was sitting on one of the chairs, she momentarily forgot about Matt and the complication of Joe's insisting she deserved the promotion.

"Problem?" Joe asked.

She turned back and murmured, "Millie Jackson. I was afraid she'd be in sooner or later. I wish it had been later though."

"Jackson. The husband passed away a few months ago, right?" Joe asked. "I remember seeing the paperwork on the account taxes."

"Yes, he did," Liz replied in a quiet voice. "Financially, her farm is in a very precarious position." She smiled wanly. "Joe, how the hell do you tell a person that no matter how you jiggle and juggle the finances, the only probable option is to sell the family farm before there's real trouble?"

Joe smiled and patted her shoulder. "You're worrying for nothing, Liz. This is exactly the kind of situation in which you shine. Knowing you, you'll find the perfect solution for the woman. I expect it'll be something especially creative this time too. Millie Jackson has nothing to worry about with you in her corner. Well, I better be going."

As Liz said good-bye to him, she wished she had the confidence Joe had in her ability to help Millie. The only sensible and practical solution she could see was for Millie to sell the farm.

Realizing she couldn't put Millie off any longer, she forced a smile to her lips and turned to the woman. Millie returned the smile with a nervous one of her own.

"Hello, Millie," Liz said, gesturing for the woman to come to the desk. "I'm sorry to keep you waiting."

"That's okay, Liz," Millie replied, rising and scurrying over to sit on the edge of a visitor's chair. Millie was in her late fifties, rail-thin, her face lined by a lifetime of perseverance and hard work.

As Liz walked back to the desk, she took a deep breath and steeled herself for the coming interview.

Five minutes later, the discussion every bit as painful as she'd suspected, Liz hesitated, not wanting to tell Millie that her best option was to sell the farm. She searched her mind for *any* other way she could change the reality of the situation for Millie. Nothing came.

"It isn't the debts, Liz," Millie protested before Liz could gather the right words to make the truth more palatable. "Even if the farm were making money, I just don't think I could do even the managing. My girls are telling me to sell out, and my head tells me that they're right. But the whole idea of selling just breaks my heart."

"I know. But I think your girls are right," Liz said in a gentle voice. She knew she was doing the best thing by agreeing with Millie's children, but she still felt like a rat for it. There had to be something she'd overlooked. Something . . .

When they'd ended their discussion and Millie finally left the bank, Liz realized Joe was right. She'd never forget customers like Millie Jackson. No bank manager worth her salt could. Why *couldn't* she find that financially creative something that would allow Millie to keep her farm? Even though Millie herself seemed resigned to selling out, Liz still felt as if she were letting the widow down—and Joe too. Clearly Joe had meant only to be encouraging about her interview with Millie. But she couldn't help feeling as if he were depending on her to come up with a solution for Millie that would dazzle the bank's board of directors, so that they had no option but to give her the promotion.

Liz felt a huge, invisible vise clamping down on her, allowing no relief for the pressures building inside. Nothing had been settled with Matt. Joe was expecting the impossible from her. And now Millie.

Th urge for a cigarette stronger than ever, she yanked open her bottom desk drawer, where she kept her purse. She didn't even care if she was backsliding again as she took out a pack of cigarettes and matches. She lit a cigarette and inhaling deeply. While blowing out the smoke, she looked around for an ashtray and remembered why there wasn't one. She had never allowed herself or the tellers to smoke while working.

"I'm taking a break," she announced to Georgina and Mavis. Their eyes even wider because of her unusual behavior, they nodded.

"If I'm not back in ten minutes, I've gone quackers," Liz added, and walked out the door.

Ten

"We've got to stop meeting like this, Callahan."

Matt's head jerked up at the sound of a voice coming from where he'd least expected it. He'd been carefully squeezing his way through the hole in the side hedge, and now sharp twigs scratched his face and stabbed viciously at his belly.

"Dammit, Liz! What the hell are you doing out here at this time of night?" he grumbled while scrambling the rest of the way through the hedge. Silently he vowed to cut a nice big square in the boxwood, put in a gate, and to hell with any gossip. Crawling around on the grass like a two-year-old was ridiculous.

"I'm pondering the meaning of life," she said in answer to his question. "And I've decided it's the pits. Have a cigarette?"

There was no moon, and he could barely make out her shadow in the darkness even though she was sitting against her garden shed less than two feet away from him. Unfortunately he couldn't miss the small red glow that seemed to dance all by itself as Liz raised a cigarette to her lips.

"I gave up cigarettes when I was sixteen and realized they wouldn't make me any tougher than the rest of the guys in the street gang I belonged to," he said. He sat down next to her and leaned his back against the shed's flimsy steel side. "When are you going to give up the things?"

"I hate secure people," Liz said, taking another puff of the cigarette. "You'd probably be able to tell Millie Jackson to sell her two-hundred-year-old farm and not even flinch at all the years and memories she'd have to give up just because it's best for her."

Realizing Liz needed comfort and that he'd been lecturing at her again, Matt swore silently. He had heard Millie Jackson had been widowed just before he moved to Hopewell. Liz had had an extremely bad day, and she obviously was agonizing over it. Feeling like an ogre, he snatched the pack of cigarettes out of her hand, took one, and stuck it between his lips. "Gotta light?"

She chuckled dryly, then pulled the cigarette from his lips and crumbled it into pieces. "I won't lead someone else astray. It was only a momentary lapse when I offered you a cigarette. From now on, leave the vices to me."

"And you do them very well," he said, placing his arm around her shoulders and settling her against his side. She wore a heavy sweater and jeans, and he resigned himself to the bulky wool that separated his hands from her silky skin. "You have your cigarette, honey. Foreclosures must really be rough."

"It isn't a foreclosure, thank goodness." She sighed. "Millie's a widow, and she can't keep up the farm by herself. What she needs is someone to manage the farm and hands to do the work, but she won't get either without a dependable cash source. And farms work on speculation, which is borrowing from the bank and crossing your fingers that you can pay the money back. I ought to know, since I see more crossed fingers than money from the farmers."

"What's a nice girl like you doing in the banking business?" he asked quietly, and kissed her temple. He'd never realized before how much Liz loved the people in the area and wondered if they knew it.

"I like money and I like people, and I love pulling some strings to help them. My boss says that's why I'm good at my job." There was a short silence, and even though his eyes were adjusting to the black night, he sensed her wry grin more than saw it. "It makes me feel as if I've beaten the system on its own terms. I should be beating the system for Millie, dammit!"

Hearing the desperation in her voice, Matt instantly sought to dispel it. "You can't be superbanker all the time. You told Millie what you really thought was best for her, right?"

Liz leaned back against his shoulder and nodded.

"Then you did your best for her."

She flicked the half-smoked cigarette onto the ground and it disappeared under her sneakered foot as she extinguished it. "You're probably right.

But Millie wants to stay on her farm. And I ought to be able to figure out how to help her do that. The solution is there, I just know it, but somehow I can't see it!"

"Honey, stop torturing yourself," he said, stroking her back to soothe her. "You know you can't help everybody, so think of the ones you have helped, like Micah Davis—"

"You heard about that, eh?" she broke in with a genuinely amused chuckle.

He laughed. "You think you can throw a bull named Romeo at me and I'm not going to ask?" He became serious again. "You helped a man make a comeback with his livelihood when he thought he'd lose everything. People in this town are still talking about how much you helped him. I'm sure nobody expects Millie to try to run her farm by herself, and nobody expects you to run it for her. You advised her to *her* best interests, and that's what's important."

Liz sighed, and he could easily hear that he had not convinced her.

"You were in a street gang?" she asked suddenly.

Matt couldn't help grinning at the instant and unexpected change of subject. He'd almost forgotten he'd mentioned his childhood in his attempt to shame her into putting out the cigarette. While that hadn't succeeded, at least Liz had momentarily forgotten Millie Jackson.

"I was just a dumb kid," he said in dismissal, feeling a sudden reluctance to talk about a time long past and better forgotten. "I'd rather talk about you and—"

"Do you realize I don't know anything about

you as a boy?" she asked, turning around until she was facing him.

Her hip curved naturally into his own, and her breasts pressed distractingly into his chest. But it was her mouth bare inches from his that made him forget what he was going to say. He bent his head—

Her elbow suddenly dug into his side.

"Ouch!"

"Serves you right." She tried to sound cross. "We were talking about you."

"Us," he corrected her, sliding his hands underneath the sweater. His fingers automatically smoothed their way up her warm flesh to unsnap her bra. "You don't need this."

He received another elbow in his ribs for his efforts.

"Dammit Liz!" he exclaimed, rubbing his side.

"Talk," she ordered as she resettled herself against him.

"I was just a dumb kid, that's all. Can I kiss you now?" he asked, hoping she'd be satisfied with his short answer.

She wasn't. "If you were just a dumb kid, then why don't you tell me about it? Or maybe you have something to hide. Like a jail sentence. Good Lord! Did you kill someone in a gang fight?" she teased.

A chuckle escaped him. "You've got one hell of an imagination, honey. It was nothing like that. I just got in with a bad crowd until I wised up. The worst things I ever learned were to cut school, smoke, and how to hot-wire a car in under three minutes."

Liz burst out laughing.

"Shh!" he hissed almost reluctantly as the sound seemed to boom in the night air. He loved the sound of her laughter, but someone might hear her, and he had no wish for her to be discovered in an embarrassing position with him. And if her small but fully-rounded breasts kept jiggling against his chest as they were doing at the moment, Liz would find herself in more than an embarrassing position. She'd find herself naked and underneath him.

To his relief and disappointment, her laughter subsided into a fit of giggles and she finally gasped out, "But I did that stuff, too, as a kid."

"You stole cars for the chop shops?" he asked in disbelief, and immediately wished he'd never voiced the too revealing question.

Her jaw dropped in clear astonishment. "You stole cars with a gang!"

"I started several cars without keys," he flatly admitted as his hands automatically dropped away from her. "And none of them were mine. Then I realized how stupid it was and got out, okay?"

She suddenly rose up on her knees and wound her arms around his shoulders.

"Oh, Matt," she murmured as she pressed his head to her breast.

He mistook the concern in her tone for pity, and it infuriated him. He pushed her arms away and scrambled to his feet.

"You want to feel sorry for me, then fine! Here's the whole story. I have no idea who my father was, and my mother dropped me on the welfare office doorstep when I was a baby. I had a foster mother who was good to me, but she died when I was sixteen, and the next home wasn't so good, so I ran away and lived on the streets, pushing myself into more and more trouble. It wasn't long before I realized how stupid I'd been to take out my hurt on the world. I had no skills and no diploma other than the kind you get on the streets. And that's where you stay if you don't have anything else. So I bugged a modeling agency for a job because I thought the work was easy and because everyone called me 'pretty boy.' They finally gave me one. Now I live happily ever after in Smalltown, U.S.A., where I always wanted to belong. End of *Oliver Twist*, okay? I don't want your pity, and I'm sorry as hell I even brought the subject up!"

Sleepless hours later in his lonely bed, Matt realized he'd never given Liz a chance to speak before he'd scrambled back through the hedge and into the house. And if she had spoken, he doubted he would have listened at the time. He'd been too angry—and afraid that he'd lost her respect. Logically he knew she'd already been upset about Millie Jackson having to sell her farm, so it was understandable that she'd have compassion for a boy headed for self-destruction. If their lives had been reversed, he'd probably feel the same for her. The past shouldn't matter anymore. It hadn't mattered for a long time. Maybe he'd subconsciously avoided telling her because of what had happened with her ex-husband. But he just couldn't shake the feeling that it was important to wipe away that moment of pity from Liz. Only how?

He discarded several sudden wild ideas, and as he did, he found the problem of Millie Jackson intruding on his consciousness. Liz had said the woman needed manpower and a constant cash flow to keep up her farm. He had moved to Hopewell because he'd always wanted to live in a place where the people cared about one another. Maybe it was time to show Liz he cared as much as she did, by helping Millie. If he did something to earn the town's respect, it should be more than enough to wipe out his disreputable past.

Mulling over how good it would feel to have Liz back in his arms, he finally drifted off to sleep.

Backing her car out of her driveway and slowly cruising past Matt's house, Liz frowned with worry when she saw that the living room drapes were still closed and the Corvette was still missing from the driveway.

"Seven days," she muttered out loud, and pressed down heavily on the gas. The car lurched forward, and she instantly eased off the pedal, slowing to a normal speed.

Grimacing, she remembered how Matt had disappeared the morning after their argument. She hadn't been able to get an apology in edgeways. It was all his fault that she had felt sorry for the teenage Matt. If he'd been a demanding male, all bellows and orders, she would have gladly called the police to check on the statute of limitations. But no, he had been tender and understanding with her, so naturally, when she'd heard about his deprived childhood, she'd felt an overwhelming rush of love and sympathy. She'd never considered not expressing them.

And he'd rejected her.

More than that, he was gone.

She drove automatically as she wondered if he knew how proud she was of him for the tremendous odds he'd overcome to become successful and wealthy. No wonder he'd retired so young! He must have worked himself almost to death to attain the goals he had, and in so short a time. She'd always had a lovely family to support her during the bad times, but Matt had had nothing and no one.

Nothing and no one then, but now he had her.

At least he would, she silently vowed, if he ever came back from wherever it was he had gone.

And if he didn't, she'd look for him no matter how long it took. Then she'd tell him the last thing she felt for him was pity, and that she loved him. And if he still refused to come back home, she'd drag him by his beard.

It was late afternoon when the bank's doors opened unexpectedly. Liz glanced up sharply from the tellers' daily receipts lying on her desk, realizing Georgina had forgotten to lock the front doors again after closing. She *should* have checked. . . .

All thought ceased, and she gasped in astonishment as Matt strolled inside with Millie Jackson.

"Oh, Liz, I'm so happy," Millie blurted out as she rushed past the open gate of the wrought-iron divider separating the tellers' area from the manager's.

Liz's astonishment doubled when Millie turned frankly admiring eyes to Matt, who had stopped on the other side of the divider. He smiled charmingly at Millie, then turned to Liz.

She stared in confusion at the two of them. Matt was very pleased about something, and it obviously involved Millie. Of all the ways she had hoped for him to reappear, this was definitely not one of them.

"Matt has found a way for me to keep the farm without worrying about money and such," Millie gushed. "And I wanted you to be the first to know."

"What?" Liz finally managed to ask.

"Matt heard about my . . . ah . . . problem." Millie giggled at her euphemism before continuing. "He's arranged for a private foundation to lease the farm as a kind of vacation home for underprivileged children. The foundation will see to the daily running of the farm, since their whole idea is to provide the children with the stability of farm life, even if it's only for a few weeks. And the children will learn how nature and humans depend on one another."

As Millie gave a long speech on the virtues of country living, Liz's mind was working away. Of course it would all sound wonderful to Millie. She'd do anything to keep her farm.

"Which foundation?" Liz interrupted in a cool tone while clasping her hands in front of her on the woodgrain Formica desktop.

"The Deerling Foundation," Matt replied, his smile slowly fading.

And well it should, Liz thought, still a bit confused by the turn of events. But she knew she couldn't find fault with the Deerling Foundation; it was a reputable one.

She turned to Millie. "Your intentions are wonderful, but I think you should consider this very carefully, Millie. It will be a big change for you, with the constant disruption of strangers coming and going all the time. While the farm will still be yours, you must realize also that there may come a time when the foundation might want to do something with the farm that you won't like. And sometime in the future they might have to institute some cost-cutting measures and your farm might be one of them. Then what will you do?"

"Well . . ."

Matt spoke smoothly over Millie's hesitation. "The foundation has guaranteed Millie the right to dissolve the project at any time she wishes within the first two years. After that they will lease the farm for ten years, while still giving her a *yearly* option to dissolve the project. As you can see, the foundation is well aware of *who* actually owns the farm. They are not concerned that the farm be a paying operation, but that the children have an environment to learn respect for themselves and others."

Liz felt her cheeks heating, and she suppressed the embarrassment rising inside her. She firmly told herself that she was only pointing out a few of the project's pitfalls to Millie. She was *not* feeling humiliated because she hadn't come up with a way to help the woman and Matt had. Pride had nothing to do with it. Someone should remind Millie of potential trouble, that was all. She was simply that someone.

"I know it's exactly what Luther would want me to do," Millie said defensively, breaking into Liz's thoughts. "He always said he never wanted to sell, especially to these new farming conglomerates."

"Nobody wants you to do that," Liz hastily assured the woman. She swallowed back a lump of pride. "This really sounds like a wonderful project. I just didn't want you to rush into anything without carefully considering all the facts first." She swallowed back a second and much larger lump. "Mr. Callahan should be commended for finding another option for you."

"Matt said I should think it over carefully, just like you did," Millie admitted, smiling sheepishly. "And I am thinking carefully before I sign the papers. I guess I just got excited that I could keep the farm going without the worry. I really didn't want to sell, you know."

Liz gave the woman a polite smile. She refused even to look at Matt.

Millie went on. "You were so concerned for me that day I came in to see about the loans that I wanted you to be the first to know my good news."

"Thank you, Millie. I'm very glad to hear it," Liz answered with all the graciousness she could muster. She forced herself to turn toward Matt. "Congratulations, Mr. Callahan. This looks very promising for Millie, and I hope she and Deerling can work out a successful arrangement."

Matt's brows were drawn together in a puzzled frown as he stared at her. "Thanks. Millie? Would you mind waiting in the car for a few moments? Since I'm here I'd like to talk to Liz about my account, and then I'll drive you home, okay?"

Millie nodded and said a cheery good-bye that Liz barely heard. She was too busy forming her first question. The door to the bank swung close with a whoosh, signaling her battle charge.

"How could you?" Liz began, her brain scrambling to sort through all that had just happened.

"What? What?" Matt stuttered in astonishment. "What are you so angry about?"

"You," she shouted as she shoved back her chair and jumped to her feet. "I worry myself half to death all week wondering where you are and whether you're coming back. I don't know what I did to upset you like that, and you never gave me a chance to apologize! Well, the hell I will, Matt Callahan! Not after what you just put me through."

"But I thought you'd like it," he said in a confused voice. He started to walk around the divider.

"Stay right where you are!" she ordered him. He stopped, gazing at her with growing frustration. "Oh, I like it all right, Callahan. I like never receiving a phone call to tell me where you are, let alone what you're doing. And I love the humiliation of crying on your shoulder about Millie, and you never opening your mouth to say: 'I've got a great idea, and what do you think, Liz?' "

"I wanted—"

"Let me speak! You've yelled at me, and when you weren't yelling, you were kissing me. You turned my emotions upside down until I was a dish of Jell-O. You made me risk my job and my promotion by making me act as crazy as you do." She shook a finger at him, not caring what she said just as long as she said it. "Well, let me tell you something, Matthew Callahan! You'd better find some other village idiot to fall in love with you, because I have had enough! Now, please leave!"

"Liz!"

"Just get out!"

Angry and hurt, she unthinkingly stalked past the open gate in the divider and out the front door.

Eleven

"He made a fool of me," Liz muttered without a glance at where she was going. She clenched her hands into tight fists. "He's been making a fool of me ever since he moved next door! Of all the humiliating things to do to a person! That was the final straw."

Still muttering out loud, she was across the town's common and halfway down Lincoln Street before she began to calm down, and she remembered *Matt* was supposed to have made the grand exit from the bank.

"Great, *just* great! *damn, daaammmnnn!*" she wailed, jerking to a halt in front of Hopewell's only church.

She covered her face with shaking hands. Of all the dumb, idiotic things to do, she thought frantically. How could she have been so stupid? Matt was probably back at the bank, laughing his fool head off.

"Oh, Lord!" she gasped in horror. "The bank!"

She whipped around and started running back up Lincoln Street, shame momentarily giving way to panic at the thought of having left the bank unattended. At the corner of Lincoln and the common, she skidded to a second, even more abrupt halt, one of her heels catching in a crack in the sidewalk. She tripped once before catching herself and straightening.

If she were *very, very* lucky, he wouldn't have left, she thought. But then she would have the humiliation of facing him after doing something so stupid.

She looked across the common for Matt's car. She instantly stopped herself.

"I don't want to know," she whispered, closing her eyes.

Realizing that Matt was a responsible citizen, and knowing in her heart that he'd never leave her in such a predicament, she snapped her eyes open and looked across to the bank.

The Corvette was still in front of the bank's red brick facade, but evidently not for long. Panic and relief washed through her when she saw Matt striding around the front of the car.

Surprised that he'd leave the bank empty and unlocked before her return, she ran as fast as she could across the street and onto the common. Absently hitching her straight skirt of beige linen up her thighs with one hand, she ran impossibly fast until she almost flew over the grass. She didn't even bother wasting time or breath by shouting to get his attention.

But before she could reach him he was inside

the car. It immediately roared to life, and with a squeal of tires, zoomed away from the curb to disappear around the corner.

While crossing the street on the other side of the common, she wondered in disbelief how he could leave the bank like that.

She'd never seen signs of his irresponsibility before, she realized. Had he been irresponsible all along, but she'd been too intrigued by his crazy charm to see it? When she'd needed him to cover for her, he'd let her down. He knew that she was responsible for whatever happened at the bank, and he'd just up and left.

Reaching the bank's double doors, she yanked the right one open and half-ran inside . . . and skidded to a stop at the sight of Mr. Seaver, the postmaster, smiling kindly at her from one of the lobby chairs.

"Everything okay now?" he asked, rising to his feet.

Huffing, she stared at him and nodded.

"Good," he said. "Matt told me you thought you'd left your car radio on. I did that one night— funny, how you forget about those things, isn't it? Didn't hurt the battery though. You shouldn't have any problem, Liz. I was a little surprised that you came back in through the front instead of the back."

"The back?" she repeated while trying to calm herself enough to think properly. Matt must have seen her car wasn't in front and used it as an excuse to explain her absence. Grateful that Mr. Seaver evidently hadn't noticed she'd walked to work that morning, she took a deep breath and replied. "Oh. The back. The door locks automatically, and I never thought to take the keys." She swallowed and asked, "Where's Matt?"

"Millie wasn't feeling well, and he wanted to get her home. I just happened to be passing by on my way home from the post office, and he asked me to wait for you. Been nice and peaceful, you'll be glad to know."

"I see." She tried to smile. "Thanks, Mr. Seaver. I really appreciate it."

He chuckled. "Can't have anyone robbing the bank while you're not here. I better be going, so you can get home yourself."

After the elderly man had left, Liz firmly locked the doors and patted them in relief. She checked to make sure everything was in order in the bank, that the time vault had been locked and set. Then she gathered up her things from her desk and made her way to the back door. Stepping into the warm afternoon sunlight, she closed the door behind her, smiling to herself as it gave a satisfying click.

Her smile faded when she caught sight of the empty employee parking spaces behind the bank. Matt had left her a shred of dignity when he'd had Mr. Seaver watch the bank, she thought, slowly walking down the asphalt-covered alley. But he hadn't left her much else. No pride, no common sense. No love.

She moaned, hoping the sudden, vague memory she had of her telling him to find somebody else to fall in love with him was a figment of her imagination. "Oh, Lord, I didn't! I couldn't have!"

But she heard herself shouting at him to "find

some other village idiot to fall in love with you" as clearly as she could hear the DeNato children playing in their backyard on the other side of the alley. Of all the things she could have said, she had said that! Her face flamed scarlet as her mind instantly replayed the whole scene, even to the details of the baby blue T-shirt Matt had worn under his raw silk blazer. And the terrible hurt returned as she remembered her days of worry while he'd been gallivanting around like a white knight on his faithful charger to save Millie's farm.

She should have been on that charger herself! At least she should have been on it with him, she corrected herself reluctantly. But the man had used her. She had shared her concerns with him, and he had tossed them away as if they had been a late notice from the phone company. Could she forgive that?

Liz walked the rest of the way home. And as she did, her pride never allowed her to spare a glance at the profusion of blooming roses in almost every garden.

Less than twenty-four hours later Liz blessed that little shred of dignity Matt had given her yesterday. It had played on her conscience all evening while she sat barricaded in her house. It had niggled at her all morning during the monthly meeting at the bank's central office in Swanton.

Now, as she drove along the lonely country road on her way back to Hopewell, she had nothing to do but think. To her left, behind a low stone wall, cows grazed under the late July sun. On the right, in straight, furrowed rows, the future harvest sprouted. An occasional copse of trees in full green foliage broke into the endless vista of rolling hills. In the distance the razor-sharp peaks of the Green Mountains rose up in a natural barrier, separating one side of Vermont from the other.

Liz usually found the scene soothing, but she realized that it wasn't helping her now. Her mind was too full of Matt.

With a grimace she decided Matt *should* have been the one waiting for her at the bank. She had deserved the full and total humiliation of slinking back to face his laughter. Then she wouldn't be feeling this tremendous guilt.

"The clown who said, 'Pride goeth before a fall,' at least could have mentioned how high the cliff was," she muttered, then sighed in despair.

Matt had unselfishly given help where she couldn't, but she'd been too proud to acknowledge that fact. It had taken all night and most of the morning before she'd finally realized how juvenile she'd been the day before.

How selfish and ungrateful she must have sounded yesterday. From the beginning Matt had always considered her feelings, had understood the things that were important to her. He'd made every effort to give her time to accept what had been happening between them. He'd asked only that she not shut him out.

Such a small request, Liz thought. And one she'd disregarded from the beginning. A modern woman had every right to demand a man treat her as his equal, in business and in love. But she had no right to trample on the poor guy when he was doing his best in the equality department. And a modern woman ought to apologize when she recognized how unfairly she'd treated her man.

Liz swallowed. That was the problem. It wasn't easy to apologize to Matt after she'd told him she loved him in one breath—and to take a flying leap in the next.

But she'd do it. She owed him a big apology, and if banking had taught her one thing, it was to pay her debts. It just took a little courage, she told herself, while her insides shrank at the thought. She'd do it tonight, right after work. On the other hand, maybe she ought to wait until tomorrow. Then she'd have all night to find the perfect words, so he'd have no other choice but to forgive her.

She made a face. Okay, so she was a first-class coward.

Her reflections were diverted by the sight of a white car parked on the side of the road by the stone wall. She leaned forward and peered through the windshield, trying to make out if someone was stranded and needed help, or if it was a tourist who had just stopped to admire the view. Keeping in mind the many news stories of faked stranded motorists, she had no intention of stopping herself—she acted like an idiot only where Matt was concerned— but she would send back help if it were needed.

As she swiftly drew closer, Liz tensed. Her fingers gripped the steering wheel until her knuckles were pale. The white car was beginning to look familiar. Too familiar.

"It couldn't be!" she exclaimed in a shocked whisper.

To her dismay, she recognized Matt's Corvette. And Matt, leaning against the wall. Panic flashed through her, and she wondered wildly if she could get away with passing by as if she hadn't seen him. She knew it would be the dumbest, most childish stunt yet with him, but why break her record now?

Sternly telling herself to act like an adult for once, Liz immediately slowed her car. When she reached his car, she turned the wheel slightly and rode the grass shoulder, stopping behind the Corvette. Her courage shriveling, she reminded herself that she was a grown woman who could make a simple apology for her poor behavior. That she had confessed her love didn't matter. She'd probably lost him anyway with her infantile antics.

With monumental will she opened the car door and slid out. Matt never turned from his perusal of the empty pasture. She shut the door behind her and drew in a deep breath. It didn't help.

Trying to find a thread of bravery within her, Liz stared at his tanned, leanly handsome profile. His hair was brushed off his forehead as usual, and the brown curls glinted in the sunlight. His beard seemed redder than ever, and she knew how sensual it felt against her skin whenever and wherever he kissed her. From the side his expression was brooding, but it only enhanced his perfect features. The white T-shirt he wore outlined his spine before disappearing into a pair of faded jeans that were molded to his lean buttocks and thighs. His shoulders were hunched slightly as his sinewy forearms rested on the top of the stone wall, and she could see the bold definition of his muscles under his sun-darkened skin. The hands that had drowned every inch of her body in indescribable sensations were clasped loosely in front of him.

He was absolutely beautiful, she thought in awe. The perfect man in face and form.

She suddenly realized that lately she had been repressing her awareness of his physical appearance. Instead, she must have been unconsciously concentrating on Matt the man in the hopes of discovering inner flaws. And she'd found a few. He was arrogant, but it was a tender arrogance. He was demanding, but that was tempered by gentleness. He was stubborn to the point of exasperation, and yet he was always willing to make concessions.

Well, maybe only one, Liz admitted in a brief moment of amusement. She, unfortunately, had been stubborn enough for the both of them. Matt wasn't perfect, no human being ever was, but he was a far better person than she. A little crazy, too, but that was what she loved most about him.

Wondering what she could say to him to make up for all the hurt she might have caused and dismally hoping she'd find something in the next two seconds, she walked over to the wall and stood next to him. He still didn't give her a glance as she leaned her elbows on the wall and stared out at the pasture.

Her stomach flip-flopping, she knew it was up to her to break the tense silence. Frantically searching her blank mind, she finally blurted out the only words she could think of.

"We've got to stop meeting like this."

She instantly wished herself into a deep hole as she remembered she'd once before uttered that particular phrase to him.

"I love it when you yell at me," Matt said.

His voice sounded cold and remote. Liz felt tears welling in her eyes, and she willed herself to maintain her composure. She needed to make her apology, not weep like a baby for what she had lost. She wouldn't embarrass Matt. She just couldn't do that to him on top of everything else.

"I'm sorry about yesterday," she managed in a tight voice. "What you did for Millie was a near miracle, and I acted small and petty about the whole thing." Her voice dropped. "Thank you for getting Mr. Seaver—"

His wry chuckle interrupted her. "I wonder what Hopewell thought, seeing their banker high-tailing it across the common. Fortunately you've got the legs for it, honey."

She felt the implied insult down to her toes, but didn't say anything. Matt was entitled to be sarcastic, she thought, and she'd take the bitter medicine.

Out of the corner of her eye she saw him turn toward her. "Look at me, Liz."

She sighed quietly and turned, still keeping one elbow on the wall to hold herself upright. His face was devoid of all expression, except for the tiny movement of his beard as he clenched and unclenched his jaw.

"Sometimes," he said, "a man doesn't realize

the damage he's done until it's too late. Pride won't let him see it. I never meant to hurt you. I should have realized how you'd feel and taken steps to prevent it."

"Please, Matt," she cried out as a sharp pain sliced through her. He was clearly trying to tell her in the nicest way that he didn't feel the same way she did. She told herself she'd rather die than hear the rest of his good-bye speech. "I stopped only to apologize to you. That's all."

Blindly she turned in the direction of her car.

He grabbed her arm and pulled her back against him. "Wait a minute, Liz! I'm entitled to finish my own apology before you tell me to hit the road!"

She twisted around and stared up at him in shock. "But you were telling *me* to hit the road."

"I was not!"

"Yes you were!"

"Wait a minute, wait a minute," he said, a grin beginning to form on his lips. "Is anyone telling anyone to hit the road?"

"This anyone isn't," she replied, and started laughing as he lifted her off the ground in a tight hug.

She wound her arms around his neck and buried her face in his shoulder to hide her happy tears.

"Liz, Liz," he murmured, planting kisses in her hair.

Matt covered her lips in a searing kiss, letting the special magic that was Liz flow through him. He touched her everywhere to be sure she was really there in his arms, that he hadn't lost her through his stupidity. He felt her hands burrow into his hair, trying to pull him closer. Her mouth was infinitely soft and sweet as it fused with his. Her tongue darted into his mouth, challenging his to a gentle duel. As she wrapped her arms more tightly around him, he felt himself beginning to fall under her irresistible spell. Then he suddenly remembered they were out in the open and anyone could pass by and see them.

Reluctantly he let her go. By some miracle he hadn't ruined everything, but he wouldn't press his luck any further.

Seeing her open, unfocused gray eyes, he smiled. The freckles that dotted her delicate gamine features were becoming more prominent from the summer sun. Her wheat-colored hair was loose around her shoulders, and was streaked with white-gold highlights he'd never noticed before. It must be the sun, he thought, and reached out to touch it, savoring the feel of the silken strands clinging to his fingers. He couldn't help smiling at her pastel green blazer, dirndl skirt, and the white blouse with its Victorian collar and ruffled jabot. His Liz was as prim as always on the outside, and only he knew about the simmering volcano underneath.

"I wasn't pitying you," she said in a determined tone.

"That's debatable," he rushed in before she could say more. He chuckled. "But it took a while for me to realize your feelings weren't directed at me, but at a young, mixed-up boy who's long gone now."

She nodded. "Exactly. Why did you take off like that, without a word?"

He rolled his eyes heavenward. "You would ask that. I wanted to surprise you by helping Millie."

She grinned. "Believe me, I was surprised. It just took me a while to be delighted."

"I eventually realized I'd jumped all over you for nothing that night when we were sitting by the garden shed," he continued, wanting to clear up the mess he'd made with her. "That night also made me realize how lucky I had been. Suddenly I knew I wanted to give some other kids a chance for a better life. A chance I had never had. So I went to New York and saw the head of the Ford Modeling Agency. My former employer has always been involved in charity work, and she's on the board of Deerling. She liked my idea of a working farm project, where the children could learn about responsibility and self-respect. Besides, I had a crazy notion that if I helped Millie, I'd be a respectable citizen in your eyes."

Liz started laughing. "Matt, you have never been a respectable citizen to me. Just crazy. And I love you for it."

"You'd better," he growled, then gave her another searing kiss. Finally he murmured against her pliant lips, "I love you, Liz."

"I love you, you crazy nut."

There was a long moment of silence, then Matt raised his head and said, "I think I always have loved you. You're beautiful and sexy as hell. You're independent and stubborn. You're dynamite in a tiny, primly wrapped package. You're a fighter just like me, although you've been fighting the wrong things for a while now."

"Don't ruin it," she warned him dryly, leaning back on his arm that was curved around her waist.

He chuckled and kissed her again. "See. Still fighting. What you need is someone to control you, woman! What you need is a man—"

"Too bad I can't find one," she said, looking everywhere but at him.

He tugged at her hair until her amused gaze settled back on his face. "You're in terrible shape, honey. I never should have allowed you the upper hand in this relationship."

"Just a momentary slipup on your part, I'm sure," she murmured, curling her arms around his neck. She pressed her body full against him. "Welcome back, Macho Man."

Matt smiled at the name. At the moment he felt more powerful, more secure in his maleness than ever. Love made a person stronger, not dependent, he thought. It defined the individual halves while forming two people into a whole. It provided support, caring, forgiveness, and shelter. A tiny private world against the hurts of the larger one. He realized there was a tremendous strength for a man in loving a woman and being loved in return. And he would nurture this love, protect it.

He gathered Liz closer, wanting to seal their commitment physically.

A distant enraged roar and pounding hooves suddenly shattered the poignant silence.

"What the hell—"

"Run!" Liz screamed, pulling at his arm while obeying her own order.

As he turned toward the cars, Matt glanced over his shoulder and caught a glimpse of a four-legged monster the size of a freight train bellowing its anger. The thing sped toward them from over a hillock at the other end of the pasture, closing the short hundred yards in shockingly few seconds.

"Holy—"

Matt bit off the curse. His heart slamming against his chest, he grabbed Liz by the waist and raced for the meager protection of the cars. He fervently prayed the stone wall would hold the creature back long enough for him to get the Corvette started.

"Hide on the other side while I get the keys out!" he shouted, giving Liz a push toward the front bumper when they reached the car.

"It's okay," she said, gasping as she grabbed his arms. She started laughing. "It's only Romeo."

"Are you crazy?" he yelled over the bull's loud bawling. "That thing could easily break through the wall!"

"I don't think so," she replied breathlessly, and pointed back to the stone barrier. "Anyway, he won't."

Matt turned and watched in surprise as Romeo, still complaining noisily, paced back and forth on the other side of the wall. He made no attempt to push against the wall or scale it, seemingly content with scaring ten years out of his victims.

"I thought we were goners," Matt muttered, realizing Romeo was quite a bit smaller than he'd first thought. He'd always pictured the animal as being more the size of the famous black Andalusian bulls of Spain. Of course, Romeo wasn't exactly a toy poodle either.

"Micah must have just let him into the pasture," Liz said. "The gate's on the other side. I'm sorry, Matt. I guess I forgot exactly where we were."

"It's okay. Are you sure he won't come through the wall?" Matt asked dubiously, eyeing the short horns that still looked wicked enough to rip a man open in one swipe.

"Romeo is very protective of his territory, but he doesn't overstep his boundaries," Liz replied with a chuckle. "He might be a dairy bull, but he's got an oversized ego where strangers are concerned. Unfortunately Micah never had the heart to have Romeo dehorned when he was a calf, and now it's too late."

"As one macho male to another, I can certainly respect Romeo wanting to protect what's his," Matt said dryly. "And I don't intend to take chances with mine. Let's get the hell out of here."

Twelve

As she waited patiently in the darkness of her living room, Liz chuckled, remembering the way Matt had almost shoved her into his car that afternoon. Romeo had certainly made his usual awe-inspiring first impression.

Her amusement faded as she realized the bull had disrupted them before they had finished their discussion. There were still a few minor obstacles to be worked out—like how to go public and when. She and Matt had never even had a first date. In her zeal for privacy, she'd forced Matt to use more devious methods in his courtship of her. Now, of course, things were different.

Curling her feet up under her on the swivel rocker, Liz wondered how slowly they should take their public dates. She had the feeling neither of them would be satisfied with that arrangement for very long. About two minutes, probably. Maybe a whirlwind courtship would be better.

There was only one problem with that, she decided in growing frustration. A whirlwind courtship always ended in a quick marriage. Matt had never mentioned marriage.

Hearing the click of the back door opening, Liz dismissed her doubts. She'd simply ask him what was next . . . and throw him back to Romeo if marriage wasn't in there somewhere.

"You're making it easy on your 'secret admirer,' " Matt said in a low voice as he entered the living room.

"Aren't you glad?" she murmured, rising out of the rocker and going into his arms.

His kiss was devastating, and Liz instantly forgot the notion she'd had of talking. She groaned as his hands found her breasts under the lavender satin robe she was wearing, his thumbs bringing her nipples to aching points. Slipping her own hands under his black sweater, she caressed the muscles of his back, glorying in the satin-sheathed iron.

"Lord, but you feel good. Damn good," he whispered against her soft mouth. "Bed?"

"Bed."

She curled her arms around his shoulders, and he lifted her in his embrace. As he carried her up the stairs, she felt as if he were carrying her into a tent in a desert, like a sheikh with his harem favorite. Just the two of them, and a night of love.

"Miss me?" he asked, gazing down at her exactly like that desert sheikh would.

She gave her answer in another kiss. But when she would have broken away, his hungry mouth held hers. Mists seemed to close in on her, and she clung to him, her lids fluttering down over her eyes. Her heart pounded at the sensations his kiss provoked inside her. She trailed her fingers across his shoulders, then under the collar of his sweater, loving the feel of his warm skin.

When he finally released her lips, she became aware of her surroundings and, to her surprise, discovered they were in the bedroom and she was lying on the bed. She smiled and opened her eyes.

"That was a real suave maneuver," she said in a throaty voice.

"Sheer luck I didn't kill us both on the stairs," he admitted with a husky laugh. He came down on top of her. "We're going to make up for a lot of lost nights in this bed."

"I feel another suave maneuver coming on," she said lazily as he gathered her in his arms again.

With a chuckle he rubbed his growing arousal against her thigh. "I love it when you talk dirty."

His lips came down on hers once more, and Liz pressed herself into his hard body. She clutched at him, her nails unconsciously digging into his sweater in response to the pleasure his kiss created.

"I could kiss you forever," he murmured.

She couldn't speak as he ran his tongue up her neck, then nipped gently at her ear. Hot shudders swept through her. He calmed them with gentle kisses on her brow, her cheek, her jaw. When his kisses reached her slender neck again, they grew more demanding, tenderly savaging her sensitive flesh. His mouth dropped lower. She writhed helplessly under him as he kissed her breasts through the satin robe. He lifted his head for a moment and pushed the robe off her shoulders, baring her to the waist.

Liz felt her blood turn heavy in her veins. Her breasts ached for his touch, and, as if hearing their plea, he ran his finger lightly around the soft outer flesh. It wasn't enough, and she cried out in protest.

"I almost forgot how fragile you are," he whispered. He untied the robe's sash, then coaxed it off her. "Like a delicate piece of porcelain on the outside."

"I won't break," she assured him, reaching out and pulling his sweater over his head. She pressed her hands into the silky hairs covering his leanly muscled chest.

"And dynamite on the inside," he added breathlessly as she pushed him onto his back. "With a short fuse."

"Very short, when it comes to you," she murmured, pulling herself up and straddling him. "I love you."

"I love you." He nearly groaned as her hands began stroking his chest and ribs.

Male silk, she thought in wonder as her fingers slowly drew patterns in the thick pelt of hair. To her delight, his nipple was erect and he groaned again when she traced it with a gentle finger. She bent and kissed him.

Their mouths blended fervently, sealing their commitment to each other and giving promises of the sensual delights to be had. Matt's arms wrapped her in a haven of love. Liz felt it flow into her, even as her own love flowed to him. Tears wet her eyes at the beauty of it. Then the need came like a hot rushing waterfall, pulling her under.

His embrace tightening, Matt strung kisses down her throat and chest until he captured the soft globe of one breast. He gently nipped the satiny slope, then worried at her pulsing nipple. She cried out and clung to him. She tugged at his head, desperate for his lips on her own. He resisted and took her nipple more fully into his mouth, assuaging one ache and creating another. She moaned. His hands moved down her back, over her derriere and slender thighs.

"Matt, please, please," she chanted.

"Love you, love you," he chanted back against her breasts.

His fingers found the moist velvet between her thighs, and she nearly cried out at the fire that shot through her. From a great distance she heard his moan of pleasure. The sound of it was even more erotic than what was happening to her own body. She wanted to hear it again.

With urgent hands she pushed against his shoulders until his embrace loosened. She slid down his body, stringing frantic kisses everywhere her lips could reach. She undid his belt, her fingers fumbling a little in her haste. He chuckled softly, and she glanced up.

"Impatient, as always," he said in a tenderly amused voice. "I love it."

She smiled. "Do you?"

He gasped in surprise as she very slowly pulled down the zipper of his black jeans. Leaning forward, she ran her tongue around his navel.

"Liz! Ahhhh."

She smiled again at the strangled cry, and pushed his jeans off, let her mouth drift lower. Matt gasped and clutched her shoulders. She raised her head and chuckled.

"You could kill a man doing that!" he exclaimed, pulling her up the length of his body and settling her between his hips.

Instantly he thrust himself inside her, and Liz's playfulness vanished as she felt herself enclose him in a silken cocoon. She closed her eyes at the feel of him, strong and hot. He gripped her thighs as he began to move, thrusting upward. She met each movement of his in a delicate counterpoint. His heart beat wildly under her hands, and her own pounded just as frantically. As the pace quickened, her body quickened. Sensations tugged at her until she was twisting and turning helplessly. And through it all she could feel the love fiercely bonding them together and demanding the final commitment of man and woman. She surrendered to it in the same moment Matt did. Crying out together, they were fused into one being, one mind, one heart, one love. The joining tightened in one supreme burst, then ebbed into a gentle but unbreakable silken chain of love.

As they snuggled together in the afterglow, Matt lazily caressed Liz's back.

"Matt? How do we go public?"

"I've been wondering that myself," he said, then added forcefully, "I love you, and I want to marry you."

Very gently he kissed her. She sighed. "How about a whirlwind courtship tomorrow and a quick wedding the day after?"

He chuckled and kissed the tip of her nose. "Don't tempt me, woman. But I'm afraid this will have to be handled delicately. I don't want to cause any talk about Hopewell's upstanding banker."

"Naturally not," she agreed in a very innocent voice. "That's why you've parked your car in my driveway, made all those 'innocent' remarks in front of my tellers, and mowed my lawn. If you had been any more subtle, I would have been in real trouble."

Giving an exasperated groan, he lightly slapped her bottom. "You *would* bring that up." He grew somber. "But I think we should take it slowly. A little more open talking over the hedge during the daytime. The occasional dinner . . ."

"And how long will that take before we get around to marriage?" she asked eyes narrowing as she gazed up at him. "A year? Two? Three?"

"No! Three or four months at most, probably. Now, don't lose your temper," he added when she stiffened in his embrace. "I've heard how people in this town talk, and I'm not about to expose you to it. As you just pointed out to me, I did more than enough damage in the beginning. I won't add to it. We'll be seen talking a little more, have a few dates, and announce our engagement. By the way, is the Hope diamond big enough for an engagement ring? Or something more the size of California?"

Relaxing, she chuckled and shook her head. "I don't need a diamond ring. And certainly not one the size of a grapefruit . . ."

Her voice trailed off, and to his puzzlement, he began laughing.

"I didn't think the joke was that funny," he said, cocking an eyebrow.

She sobered, although an occasional unladylike snort escaped while she explained. "I was worried in the beginning about keeping my image. Especially when you came on like gangbusters."

"I seem to remember you kissing me several times before I even had a chance to pucker," he mused aloud. "Ouch!"

"Sorry," she murmured, and patted his beard in apology for having yanked on it. "I'll admit I had a little problem being around you."

He chuckled and immediately grabbed her hand as she tried to pull his beard again.

"Okay. Big problem," she admitted. "But you were right then. People will gossip no matter what we do—"

"And I refuse to expose you to any of it," he broke in.

Pulling the bedclothes around her torso, she sat up and turned to face him. Her voice stern, she said, "But you were the one who said it in the first place. And some people *will* gossip. We can't do anything about that. It was only because of Joe's retiring and my maybe being promoted that I had been worried."

Matt sat up. "What promotion?"

"You mean it isn't all around Hopewell already?" Liz asked in amazement.

"What promotion?"

"My boss is retiring in September, and he's recommended me to replace him as district manager. However, some of his superiors are having second thoughts about my age—"

"That's discrimination!" Matt shouted indignantly. "We'll sue the pants off them! Age! I'll yank all my money out right away."

"Oh no you won't!" She curled her arms about his shoulders, the spread dropping unnoticed onto her bare lap. Her tone softened to almost a plea. "Matt, darling. It's okay. I'm not upset. In spite of Joe's recommendation, I doubt I'm really in the running because of my low seniority with New England Bank. And seniority will probably be the biggest factor in the directors' decision. I guess I acted like a nut with you because I was afraid the least little thing would jinx whatever chance I do have of being promoted. And because of what happened in Chicago. I'm sorry." She kissed him. "Frankly, I'd rather have you than a promotion."

"You love me enough to throw away a chance at a good career move?" he asked in wonder.

She laughed and kissed him again. "What woman wouldn't, for you?"

"I could name millions," he murmured, caressing the smooth flesh of her back.

"Then you'll want to hang on to me, won't you?" she murmured back, spreading more kisses along his bearded jaw.

He gathered her against his chest, her head tucked under his chin. "I'll never let go. Joe's retiring in September, eh?"

"Mmmm."

"Then we'll go *very* slowly until after September." He held her in spite of her sudden struggle of protest. "I want you to have every chance at that promotion, sweetheart. And that includes your keeping your sterling reputation. Besides, you're forgetting one thing. The board of directors might not care if you dated the guy next door. But they'll very much care if you're dating a bank customer. It's only two months, my love. Two short months."

"And what if I say no? I want you more than any damn promotion, Matt."

He grinned into the deep shadows of the bedroom. "You forget, honey. I'm running this relationship now. Good thing too. You'd only make a mess of it. Ouch! Will you quit pinching me!"

She chuckled before saying in a very innocent tone, "But I was so overwhelmed by the nearness of you that I couldn't help myself, Matt. I just had to touch you."

"You're lucky I'm a sucker for a woman who's warm for my form. Ouch!"

"*Any* woman?"

"You. Only you," he assured her. "Now, where were we? Oh, yeah, I'm the head honcho here." He tenderly stroked her thick blond hair. "But I do mean it, Liz. I love you, and I'll do nothing to jeopardize your chances at the promotion. So we'll wait, okay?"

He tilted her mouth up to his, not giving her a chance to answer. Her lips were so soft, he thought. All of her was always so soft. He tried to express all of his feelings in the kiss. And to persuade her that he was right. Liz was the most important thing in his life, and he needed to show her he could be patient for a little while longer, until the promotion was finalized.

As he lifted his head, she sighed. "I have the feeling you'll be stubborn about this. Very stubborn."

He sensed the resignation in her words, and triumph shot through him.

"Dense and stubborn, that's me."

He lay back on the bed, pulling her with him for another kiss.

"And unmovable," she finally murmured, her hands tightening on his shoulders with clearly renewed passion.

"Wanna bet?" he answered, and dragged her mouth back down to his.

Thirteen

"This is ridiculous," Liz muttered under her breath as she returned Matt's polite wave with one of her own.

Continuing to walk past his house toward hers, she decided that Matt's idea of slowly building their relationship in public was on par with walking the distance of the earth's equator. It would take years!

But it was so sweet of him to do this for her, she thought as she reached her front door. So sweet. She opened the door and strode inside.

Very calmly she shut the door, then yelled, "And I can't stand it anymore!"

Tossing her purse and briefcase onto a chair, she marched upstairs to her bedroom. She stripped off the conservative white suit and royal blue blouse she'd worn to work, then yanked on jeans and sweatshirt.

She sternly told herself she should have fought

harder that night when Matt had insisted they wait until the district manager's replacement was confirmed by the bank's directors. But she'd been so touched at the time by his concern for her. And she had seen his point about her superiors frowning on her having a personal relationship with a customer—especially a customer with a major account. Unfortunately though, she hadn't realized how far Matt had intended to go to preserve her "sterling" reputation. He hadn't made a midnight visit since the night they made love and talked about how to go public. Five days! The only thing she'd had to sustain her were his daily telephone calls.

"Praise the saints for private lines," she muttered between clenched teeth as she went back downstairs to the kitchen to make dinner. "Otherwise, Matt would have nixed phone calls too."

She'd been right about a quick surprise marriage to him. That was what they should have done, she decided, banging a pot on the stove. Yes, there would have been speculation. But it would have been after the fact and therefore would have been brief and quickly forgotten, not only by Hopewell, but most likely by the bank too. Being businessmen, her superiors probably would think her marrying Matt was a wonderful way to keep his account at New England Bank permanently. Dating the bank's largest private depositor might be a no-no, but marrying him could be justified as good business, not to mention true love. Which, dammit, it was!

Banging several more pans helped cool her temper, and she wondered with bitter amusement if some unseen person was pulling an imaginary rug out from under her. It was ironic, she thought, that she and Matt had come full circle. Only this time it was Matt making noises about maintaining her pure banker's reputation. She had the feeling he'd have a good deal more control over the issue now that their roles were reversed. So far, no amount of reasoning or pleading over the telephone had swayed him. No matter what she said, Matt still insisted on keeping the intensity of their relationship quiet. And she loved him all the more for his reasons for doing it. But he was driving her crazy with his methods.

Liz gave a dry chuckle. Clearly that part hadn't changed.

"That part hasn't changed," she repeated out loud as a wild idea about their swapping roles ran through her mind.

She started laughing.

Good thing her roses were still blooming.

At midnight Liz let herself out the back door. Stopping for a moment on the top of the porch steps, she checked the dethorned rose she had tucked into the waistband of her dark blue jeans. Finding it secure she took a deep breath, pulled the navy scarf lower over her hair, and walked down the three steps. She ran across the dimly moonlit lawn. Reaching the garden shed, she headed around the side before finally stopping in front of the hole in the hedge.

She took another deep breath to calm her jumping stomach.

"We meet again," a deep voice whispered.

Liz shrieked and whirled around, banging the back of her head against the side of the steel shed.

"Owww!" she yelped, rubbing the painful spot. She focused her eyes on the voice's owner, who was standing on the other side of the hedge. "Matt! I really wish you wouldn't sneak up on me like that!"

"Well, you scared the hell out of me when I saw a shadow running across the lawn," he complained with a chuckle. "It took me a moment to realize it was you."

Dropping her arm back to her side, Liz smiled when he disappeared from view. There was rustling and grunting as he scrambled through to her side of the hedge.

He straightened and gave her a very visible grin. "I'm definitely cutting down the hedge tomorrow."

"About time," she murmured, stepping into his embrace.

She felt a shudder of longing when his lips met hers. How she had missed him—missed his warmth, missed his strong arms, missed his devastating kisses. Missed his love.

Finally he raised his head and murmured. "This is killing me."

"I know."

"I'm sorry, sweetheart. I thought I could stay away until . . . but I can't."

"Neither can I," she admitted, then chuckled. "In fact, I was bringing you a rose."

She reached between them, pulled the rose from her waistband, and handed it to him.

"You would have had a real surprise if you tried to leave this on my pillow," he said in an amused voice.

"I was banking on it," she replied, stroking his shoulders. "Matt, I can't stand not seeing you."

"I can't stand this arrangement either. But it's just a few weeks. At least that's what I keep telling myself.

"Matt—"

"Liz, do it my way. Please. I'd never forgive myself if I were the reason you were turned down for that promotion."

She sighed, not having the heart to fight him when he was so ready to blame himself. Any woman would kill to have a man like Matt, she thought. She knew he would encourage her in anything she wanted to do. Unfortunately, what she really wanted to do was exactly the opposite of what he wanted to do. She felt almost selfish for actually wanting to talk him out of this madness. But if she didn't, the weeks ahead would be sheer torture for them both.

"Matt—"

"No more arguments," he broke in, caressing her back. "Now, promise me you'll do this my way."

"Then promise me the nights."

"Liz, it's too risky. . . ."

His voice trailed away as she snuggled closer and kissed his jaw. "Promise me the nights, Matt darling."

With a loving mouth she traced his jawline, and he uttered a soft curse. But his hands tightened on her back in spite of himself.

"Why do I have the feeling I'm being sucker-punched?" he asked huskily as he pulled her to the ground.

"Because you are," she murmured.

His mouth covered hers.

As she surveyed the Friday evening customers gathered in the bank lobby, Liz found herself wishing for the thousandth time that she were with Matt. She sighed at the growing frustration inside her and suppressed it yet again. Another hour and she'd close the bank. Several hours more and maybe she'd see Matt. For a brief time.

Nothing had been resolved last night, she admitted to herself. Nothing except their obvious inability to keep their hands off each other. They had to talk—and soon. She couldn't stand the little snatches of time they had together.

" 'Evening, Liz," Fred Corliss said, breaking into her thoughts. "Busy, ain't it?"

Turning her attention to Fred, she smiled and exchanged small talk with him.

After Fred Corliss left, she realized the bank was busier than usual. Customers patiently waited three or four deep in the tellers' lines. Other customers chatted in small groups. She remembered how surprised she'd been when she'd first come to Hopewell to discover the bank was a kind of Friday night gathering place for the residents. In more heavily populated areas people were always impatient to finish their banking business and be on their way. People here never hurried. She wished she had a large dose of that patience, especially where Matt was concerned.

Another customer claimed her attention, and then she was occupied with several more who had questions about their loans or accounts. Once the rush of business was over, she glanced up and saw Matt coming through the front doors.

Forcing away the urge to run to him, she permitted herself only a polite smile. But she couldn't stop herself from rising to her feet and walking around the wrought-iron divider.

"Good evening, Matt," she said as she approached him.

He gave her a private frown for her singling him out in the crowd of people. She didn't care. She needed to be next to him, feel his closeness.

"Good evening, Liz," he finally replied.

"Is there anything I can do for you this evening?"

Liz smothered a grin when his green eyes darkened for a moment. She hadn't meant her words as a double entendre, but it didn't matter to her how he interpreted them.

"Just cashing a check for the weekend," he said loudly. "Busy tonight."

"The nights usually are," she replied impulsively, then looked around to see if anyone was paying attention to them. No one seemed to be.

"Stop it!" he muttered under his breath. Louder he said, "Well, I better get in line with the others."

"I'll be glad to cash a check for you if you're in a hurry," she said with a saccharine smile. She lowered her voice. "You've probably got a busy *night* ahead of you."

"Keep it up and it won't be," he muttered.

Chuckling quietly, she wondered how he liked being on the other side of the fence. She decided role reversal was more fun than she'd first thought.

"Actually Matt, if you've got a minute, I'd like to discuss your last deposit."

Anger blazed in his eyes, and Liz admitted that if looks could kill, she'd be dead. She knew she really shouldn't tease him.

Then again, maybe if she provoked him enough now, he'd have to make a midnight visit—if only to wring her neck.

Smiling innocently she said. "I was thinking about another type of account for you.'

"But I've already got an—"

"This is a long-term account, with a lifetime guarantee, and the occasional nine-month dividend," she broke in smoothly.

As his eyes widened at the implication of her words, she wondered what it would be like to have a baby. Matt's baby. She had a quick mental image of mischievous green eyes set in cherubic faces and little hands reaching for the cookie jar even after being told no.

More Matts to drive her crazy, she thought with wry amusement. From the look of astonishment crossing Matt's face, he obviously had never considered children. The naïveté of men. It would serve him right if she got the promotion only to take a maternity leave a few months later.

"Of course, that nine-month dividend is up to you, Matt," she added finally, deciding to ease up on him. "But it is something to consider. Would you like me to cash that check now?"

Matt glared at her, wanting to paddle her bottom then and there for nearly giving him a heart attack. At first he hadn't been sure what she'd been hinting at. A baby! He realized he hadn't thought about children before. Then he decided he'd love to see Liz nursing his child and conjured the beautiful scene in his mind. A little girl, maybe, with Liz's wheat-blond hair and gray eyes. But first he'd give Liz hell for teasing him.

"Nobody move!"

Someone screamed as Matt whipped around in the direction of the shouted order. He immediately faced two men standing in the doorway of the bank. Their faces were covered with stocking masks, and they each waved a large, very dangerous-looking gun in the air.

Acting on a long-forgotten instinct from the past, Matt threw himself against the men.

As he went down in a tangle of arms and legs with the robbers, he made a desperate grab for one of the guns as it skittered across the floor. He scooped it up at the same moment he realized he was practically sitting on one of the crooks.

He shoved the gun's muzzle into the struggling man's face and shouted, "Don't move!"

The robber stilled instantly, his harsh breathing the only noise he made. As Matt stared down at the man, he became aware of more struggling. The other crook!

Without taking his gaze off the first he bellowed, *"Somebody get the other guy!"*

To his complete astonishment it was Liz's voice that shouted back, *"I'm trying."*

He jerked his head up. The customers all seemed frozen in their places. But Liz was half-hanging on to the robber's back as she savagely clawed his stockinged face with one hand, trying to grab the man's empty hands with her other one.

Swearing viciously, Matt scrambled to his feet, yanking the first robber with him. He pushed the man against the wall, next to a small knot of people. Then he shoved the gun into the first pair of hands he found. His quick glance told him the hands belonged to Emily Richards.

"Keep an eye on this one!" he ordered her.

Emily suddenly snapped to attention and swung her bulk around to face the robber. She raised the gun to his chest and said, "Move one finger and I'll blow your head off!"

Matt barely heard her as he raced to Liz's rescue.

She was still hanging on for dear life as the second crook bucked and spun like a mechanical bronco. Out of the corner of his eye Matt saw several other men beginning to move toward them. He reached the struggling pair first, grabbed hold of the robber's jacket, and tried to find an opening to throw in a right hook. Liz was in the way.

"Dammit, Liz! I've got him!" he shouted when her nails accidentally raked his shoulder.

"He was going to shoot you!" she cried, still clinging to the robber.

"Let go!"

"You heard him, lady! Let go!" the robber shouted. "Oowww! My eye!"

"Serves you right, you creep!" Liz shouted back, beginning to pound on the robber's head. "You would have shot Matt!"

"Not me, lady!"

Matt finally gave up trying to separate the robber from Liz. Better to separate Liz from the robber before she beat the guy to death, he thought as he grabbed at her hands. He missed and received a wild fist in the eye.

"Dammit! That was me!" he shouted, this time grabbing her around the waist.

He pulled her off the robber, who instantly went down under a pile of men. Holding Liz, he stared in astonishment at the mound of humanity beside them. He suddenly realized that it couldn't have been more than ninety seconds since the robbers had entered the bank. His muscles relaxed slightly as the adrenaline began to drain out of him.

"Okay, boys, you can let him up now. Georgina, call the state police."

Matt looked over to Mr. Seaver, who had spoken. The elderly postmaster had a Dirty Harry glint in his eye as he trained the second gun with casual expertise on the robber, who was now pinned spread-eagle to the floor by a quartet of men.

Matt shook his head in disbelief.

Liz suddenly stopped squirming in his arms. She turned and sobbed into his chest. "I love you. I love you."

"Liz!"

"I don't care. I don't care. He was going to kill you."

He shook her shoulders in a desperate attempt to quiet her. "Liz! Stop it! It's all over now."

She clung harder, still sobbing. "I love you, and he was going to kill you."

"He dropped the gun!"

"He still could have killed you! Oh, Matt!"

Feeling helpless against her tears, Matt raised his head and stared at twenty pairs of bulging eyes. Hell, he thought.

"I guess she's a little hysterical," he finally said with a lame shrug.

"Hysterical!" Liz pushed out of his embrace and swiped at the tears flowing freely down her cheeks. "Hysterical! You could have been killed, tackling two robbers at once! That had to be the most stupid, the most—"

"Somebody had to stop them before they shot someone!" he shouted, glaring at her. "They would have robbed your precious bank too!"

"The hell with the bank!" she shouted back. "No damn bank, and no damn town, and no damn job is worth losing you, you idiot!"

With a sob she wrapped her arms around him again.

Hell, he thought again in resignation, holding her tightly against him. Everyone started talking at once, but he wasn't sure whether the attempted robbery or Liz had caused the most excitement. He hoped it was the robbery. With that thought he realized what might have happened if he hadn't taken the robbers by surprise. Shocked at the idea that he might have lost Liz to a bullet, he suddenly understood her hysteria.

With trembling hands he pressed her closer and murmured, "I love you, Liz. Whatever happens next, always remember that."

She lifted her tear-streaked face and whispered, "We get married, we have babies. That's what happens next. Nice peaceful boredom—if *you* can manage it."

He chuckled. "Sorry, honey. You're too exciting."

"As long as it's just me. No more heroics, ever. Promise."

"I wasn't the one clawing the guy's eyes out," he protested with amusement.

"Promise!"

He sighed. "Promise."

"Excuse me, folks."

They both glanced up to find Hank Krenshaw, the editor of the *Hopewell Bugle* smiling at them, a camera in hand. Suddenly there was a bright flash of light.

Matt blinked in confusion at the spots before his eyes.

"I saw the whole thing!" Hank said in an excited voice. "You two are the town heroes! Good thing I'm an old newspaperman and always carry my camera wherever I go. I'm giving this a front-page spread and I'm sending it in to the wire services. I bet we get picked up all over the East Coast, if not the country. I can just see the headlines—Lovers Foil Robbery Attempt!"

Matt stared at Liz in horror.

"We're public at last!" she gasped, then burst into laughter.

Epilogue

"Town heroes do not pinch other town heroes on their bottoms in public, Matthew Callahan!" Liz said sternly, and shifted in her chair as she sat next to Matt on the makeshift grandstand set up on the town's common.

"They do if they're married, Elizabeth Callahan," he replied with a sexy smile.

She sighed and clasped his offending hand in hers. "Watch the parade, darling."

"If you insist, love."

Staring at his handsome profile as he turned back to watch Hopewell's Labor Day parade, Liz sighed again. Pride and love for him filled her.

She and Matt had been married a week after the robbery, and the only argument had been over whose house they would live in. Finally she'd settled it by reminding him that he'd have to completely repack and unpack *again* if they picked her house. To her amusement, Matt had immediately insisted they live in his and rent hers furnished. And she was quite content with the decision. She'd always liked her house, but that was really all it had ever been to her—just a house. Matt, though, had bought his with the thought of building a new life for himself. She'd immediately felt at ease with his home's blending of old and new. Maybe it was because he'd made her see the old Liz within the new one. And once she'd moved in, she'd discovered how easy it was to give up cigarettes. The days were always too busy, and the loving nights provided their own habit-forming drug.

Out of the corner of her eye she saw the 4-H club pass by and remembered how the town had insisted that she and Matt be the guests of honor at the holiday festivities for foiling the robbery attempt at the bank almost a month ago. Talk about the robbery still hadn't died down, she thought. And it probably never would. It turned out there had been a third robber waiting in a car outside. The police had eventually caught him trying to cross the border into Canada. Joe, her boss, had thought the crooks had somehow gotten hold of the Brinks schedule, but the robbers had admitted they'd decided on her bank because it had seemed like easy pickings. She chuckled to herself. Of course the three hadn't known Hopewell harbored a crazy man who leaped before he thought. Matt had been hailed a hero by the town, the police, and the bank. So had she.

Everyone, though, seemed to ignore the fact that she couldn't have cared less about the bank at the time, she thought mirthfully. She'd been terrified only that the second crook would retrieve his gun before someone could stop him and shoot Matt.

Her amusement faded instantly, and she shivered in the warm sunlight. She knew she'd never forget that awful moment for as long as she lived.

"You're not watching the parade," Matt said.

"I've got something better to watch," she murmured, leaning toward him. Privately she thought he was much more interesting than the antique cars now passing the reviewing stand.

He chuckled wickedly. "Keep looking at me like that, and we'll shock the town again right here and now."

She laughed. "I think they're unshockable at this point."

"Probably. First the robbery, then you making a spectacle of yourself—"

"All in the cause of love," she broke in tartly.

"Then Millie announcing she was allowing the Deerling Foundation to use her farm for underprivileged children."

Liz tightened her grip on his hand. "I'm so proud of you for that. And what a surprise when Deerling asked you to oversee the project for them!"

Matt grimaced. "Don't remind me about my being talked into that one. Looks like my retirement's over."

"Shame on them, doing that to an old man like you," Liz murmured.

"Keep it up, and I'll pinch you again," he warned her. "Now, where was I? Oh, yes. The final shock— the new bank ads."

Laughing, she shook her head. "I don't think I'll

ever get used to seeing my face on TV or in magazines."

Someone in New England Bank's promotional department had come up with the idea of using the story of the foiled robbery in their ads. She found it very disconcerting to see a picture of herself with a bold caption underneath that read: "Earn interest with someone who will keep your money safe—bank at New England."

"It's a great ad, district manager," Matt said.

Liz grinned at him. "You know that's not official yet."

"Well, I'm just glad you got it," he replied, gazing at her with love and pride.

She smiled back.

Privately she decided she'd never forget her boss's face when he eventually discovered that Ford Carson had questioned her age only because he wanted Joe's opinion of the other managers' reaction to it. The directors had evidently taken his recommendation of her very seriously from the beginning. Funny how that worked out, she thought. All her original reasons for maintaining a good reputation had been quite valid. Yet in the end, even if she had known she all but had the promotion, she still wouldn't have cared a damn. Loving Matt and being loved by him in return were too precious to lose.

She heard the high school band strike up their opening number, and clutching Matt's hand, she pointed across the common to the uniformed musicians.

"Here comes your surprise!"

"What?" he asked in confusion.

"Just watch."

She waited impatiently through the ragged strains of "The Colonel Bogey March" as the band marched around to the reviewing stand. She'd arranged a little surprise for Matt, and now she hoped it would come off the way she'd planned. She tensed as the band reached the stand and swung into another number.

Matt frowned at her. "That sounds familiar, but I can't quite—"

"It's 'My Guy,' you nut!" she replied, then hummed a few bars along with the band. "I got them to play it for you."

"You did? What for?"

"Because I love you. You're my guy, and from now on I'm going to be talking about you to anyone who will listen."

"Sweetheart, I—"

She leaned over and kissed him, stopping his words. Finally she whispered against his lips, "I hope you like it."

"I love it," he whispered back, and deftly stroked her lips with his tongue. "And I love you."

"Mmm. By the way, being Hopewell's new philanthropist, you generously pledged the money for fifty-six new band uniforms."

His head shot up. "Liz!"

Chuckling, she sat back in her chair.

"I love it when you yell at me," she said.

And the band played on.

THE EDITOR'S CORNER

"Jolly" and "heartwarming" are words I don't hear or see nearly enough these days. That's a pity because they're wonderful words ... as well as the perfect ones to describe the quartet of romances we're publishing next month to start off the New Year with warmth and cheer.

In **DISTURBING THE PEACE**, LOVESWEPT #178, Peggy Webb gives us a worthy successor to her intense, yet madcap romance **DUPLICITY**, LOVESWEPT #157. This book is particularly well-titled because heroine Amy Logan, an inventor, truly does disturb the peace of her new neighbor Judge Todd Cunningham. Amy has a few problems perfecting her creations—like an erratic robot named Herman and a musical bed that isn't correctly programed to observe the fine distinctions between night and day. Todd is lovestruck from their first meeting, and Amy is clearly captivated by the sexy judge ... but she is also terrified of the risk he represents. Mistakenly interpreting Amy's resistance to her miscasting of him as a stuffy legal-beagle, Todd sets out to change her image of him. With a bit of assistance from Amy's zany mystery writer aunt and lots of virile charm on his own part, Todd merrily campaigns to win over the imp who has stolen his heart. A sheer delight.

Joan Elliott Pickart really outdoes herself with her next love story, **KALEIDOSCOPE**, LOVESWEPT #179. And in the secondary characters in this book, she creates two of the most delightful ladies it's been my pleasure to meet in a long, long time. Those "ladies" are devoted to liberating themselves from conventional expectations for "older people." They are also the loving mothers of our heroine and hero. Now, when these two formidable matchmaking moms plot to get their offspring introduced to each other, they do

(continued)

so in a fashion that sets the kaleidoscope of life swirling with brilliant color. Heroine Mallory Carson is a beauty and hero Michael Patterson is one gorgeous blond hunk of a divorce lawyer. Naturally Michael has seen enough of the miserable side of married life to be turned off even to the words "happily ever after," much less to believe in them. Still, he can't resist Mallory and is even drawn to her day care center, a spot he would find a most awkward one for him if Mallory was not there. Then, when the rainbow colors of love explode before the very eyes of this pair who consider themselves mismatched, they have to take the biggest chance of all.

Don't miss this wonderfully humorous and emotionally moving love story.

Patt Bucheister gives us just what every woman needs in LOVESWEPT #180, **THE DRAGON SLAYER**. She gives us a white knight in Webb Hunter. When Webb falls—literally—on and for our heroine Abigail Stout he soon decides to appoint himself her own special slayer of dragons, bringing her teddy bears and toys . . . and his promise of earth shattering passion. Abigail has been to busy with school and work and more work to have had much experience with men, so she is ill-prepared for the pursuit of Webb, who is as enchanted by her saucy personality and her beauty as he is by her most intriguing perfume: vanilla extract! Abby has learned the hard way (shunted from one foster family to another during her childhood) that happiness is fleeting and dreams do not come true . . . and she is as hard pressed to resist Webb as she is to believe in his promises. Just as you responded to Patt's first LOVESWEPT (**NIGHT AND DAY**, #130) so, too, I think, you will respond with enormous enthusiasm for this touching and memorable romance.

Is there any writer more evocative or imaginative than Fayrene Preston? Her zany cast of characters in

(continued)

ROBIN AND HER MERRY PEOPLE, LOVESWEPT #181, will worm their way into your affections just as they do hero Jarrod Saxon's. Heroine Gena Alexander has run from Jarrod whom she is convinced has betrayed her love, her trust. Starting a new life with her merry (but poor) people, Gena's eyes are opened to human suffering and to tragedy, and, like Robin Hood, she determines to do something about them. When Jarrod tracks her down and makes his intentions clear, both are jolted into an awareness of dimensions of each other that are different from any they'd ever even guessed existed. Discovery . . . joy . . . and complications because of the merry band's problems lead to Jarrod's and Gena's deep and rich revelations about the true meaning of love. This is throbbingly sensual and utterly charming romance that we believe you will long remember.

Chuckles and surprises, passion and affection abound to make for *jolly* and *heartwarming* LOVESWEPT reading next month. Enjoy!

Warm regards,

Sincerely,

Carolyn Nichols

Carolyn Nichols
  Editor
LOVESWEPT
Bantam Books, Inc.
666 Fifth Avenue
New York, NY 10103

 **LOVESWEPT**

Love Stories you'll never forget by authors you'll always remember